BURY THE CHILDREN IN THE YARD

andersen prunty

Published by Grindhouse Press
POB 292644
Dayton, OH 45429
www.grindhousepress.com

Bury the Children in the Yard: Horror Stories
Grindhouse Press #013
ISBN-13: 978-0-9849692-4-1
ISBN-10: 0984969241

This book is a work of fiction.

Also by Andersen Prunty

Satanic Summer

Fill the Grand Canyon and Live Forever

Pray You Die Alone: Horror Stories

Sunruined: Horror Stories

The Driver's Guide to Hitting Pedestrians

Hi I'm a Social Disease: Horror Stories

Fuckness

The Sorrow King

Slag Attack

My Fake War

Morning is Dead

The Beard

Zerostrata

Jack and Mr. Grin

The Overwhelming Urge

Bury the Children in the Yard

Contents

The Library of Trespass

"You get everything upstairs?" Leggy asked.

"Yep," Dump replied, tucking his feather duster into his belt. "You get everything down here?"

"Just about. You wanna help me with the library?"

"Guess so."

The auto parts factory shutting down two months ago put a lot of people out of work. Since there wasn't a lot of other work to be had, a lot of people, people like Dump and Leggy, found themselves taking jobs they wouldn't normally take. Like housekeeping. Never, at any time in either of their lives, did Dump or Leggy think they would find themselves as maids.

"Too bad the old bitch ain't here today," Leggy said, strolling across the wood floor of the living room toward the glass doors of the library on his overly long legs. Dump guessed that was probably how he got the nickname. Practically no torso and legs like two skinny trees.

"Why's that?" Dump asked. He liked to work much better when the "client" wasn't there. That way he didn't feel watched.

"Old whore usually tips pretty good."

"I guess," Dump said. Dump was a very squat man, shaped somewhat like a dumpster, and when he worked up a sweat his stink really broke open. Even he was aware of it. He couldn't imagine what other people thought. To be surrounded by that pungent, wet dog kind of smell wafting out of him regardless of how often he bathed.

"What?" Leggy said. "You couldn't use a few extra bucks. Usually enough for a six pack, at least."

"Yeah. You're right. Maybe she'll tip us more next time." Truthfully, he didn't care. He was comfortable around Leggy. If Ms. Blanchette wasn't there, that was just one less person to be around. One less person to smell his stink or look at his repellant physique.

Dump watched as Leggy, reaching the library doors, depressed the silver, antique-looking lever. A blossom of sweat had started just below the 'Happy Housekeepers' logo on his shirt.

"Maybe we shouldn't," Dump said.

Leggy, hand resting on the door lever, turned and fixed Dump with a ferocious stare. His perm had worked itself up into a frenzy and sat above those hateful looking blue eyes with a wild intensity. Leggy took his hand off the knob and twisted the waxed tips of his gray-brown handlebar mustache.

"Why the hell shouldn't we?"

"I don't know..." Dump looked at the ground, rubbed his greasy chin with his hand, the other hand fumbling with his utility belt loaded with bottles and rags and the feather duster. The feather duster was perhaps the most emasculating part about the job.

"You tell me not to do something I'd goddamn like to know why not."

"It's just... When she's here she always tells us not to go in there."

Leggy made an exasperated sigh, throwing up his arms. "Dump-o. Know what?"

"What?"

"The bitch ain't here."

"I know."

"So, if the bitch ain't gonna be here, then we're gonna do what our contract tells us to do. Which is clean everywhere in the house unless otherwise specified by the client. Well, the client ain't here to specify us not to clean in there."

Dump shuffled nervously on his thick legs, admiring the job Leggy had done on the wooden floor.

"Stop bein a fuckin candyass, Dumpy."

"Whatever."

Leggy moved closer to him.

"Look, Dump – what does Miss What's-her-face call that room?"

"The Library."

"Yeah. Of course she calls it the library." He screwed up his face and started mocking Ms. Blanchette. "'Don't go in the library.' 'Never mind the library.' 'The library's okay. Just leave it.' 'I'll get the library myself.'" He slackened his face, pulled an engraved silver flask from his jeans pocket and took a swallow. The crazy light in his eyes intensified and, after capping the flask and putting it back, he gave a couple of frisky upward tugs on his mustache. "So what *is* a library?"

Dump knew what Leggy was fishing for. Knew that was probably his whole reason for wanting to get in there in the first place. "It's a place that lets you borrow books."

"Right, my man. A library is most definitely a place that lets you borrow books. So, I guess since Miss Drycunt ain't here to give us her little tip, we might just have to borrow one of her precious books."

Dump didn't really want any part in thievery. He hated this job, hated the people he worked for, every bit as much as Leggy did, but he didn't think that gave him the right to take things from them.

"Now," Leggy said. "You gonna help me clean up in there or not?"

"I think I'm just gonna go wait in the truck."

"Aw, shit, man. You know you wanna get in there too. I mean, I ain't ever had the urge to read a goddamn thing in my life but something so shut up like that, something I ain't *supposed* to touch, well, that makes me awful eager for some fuckin learnin. Don't it you?"

Leggy had finally hit upon something that struck a chord with Dump. He had, on a number of occasions, wondered what was in that room. Maybe it was a collection of old pornography. He'd heard that some rich fucks collected that kind of thing although he didn't really see what a bunch of old shit could have that *Hustler* didn't, except the girls didn't shave their pussies back then.

Leggy could tell Dump was now interested. He turned back to the glass doors. "So you go ahead and sit out in that hot ass truck if you don't want to do what our contract states but if you want to do a good job you'll follow me on in here."

He pressed the handle down and it didn't move. "Locked," he said. "No bother. A lock ain't never stopped me before."

Dump's heart jumped around a little bit. He half-expected Leggy to take out one of the windows. Instead, he pulled a thin pick from his pocket and jabbed it into the keyhole, moving it around until he heard a click.

"Now," he said. "I ask you: if these books is so important then why the fuck don't she get a better lock?"

Dump couldn't answer him. He was sweating again. He came up behind Leggy just as the taller man swung the French doors outward.

"You smell like a fuckin outhouse," Leggy said.

"Sorry."

They entered the library together. It smelled like the one library Dump had ever been in. It was cooler than the rest of the house.

"Feels nice in here," Leggy said. "Why do those old shits always keep it so fuckin warm all the time?"

"Don't know," Dump said, eager to get his hands on one of the fat volumes lining the room.

He pulled one down. Nothing was written on the spine. Dump thought that was kind of odd. Most books, even old ones, usually had the title of the book or the author or *something* on the spine. Looking around, he noticed none of these did. But they *were* arranged, if in an unconventional manner.

The room was your standard rectangular room, probably intended to be a dining room until this book acquiring addict had taken it over and made it into something else. There was a window at the front of the house and to the left of the French doors. Except for these areas of glass (concealed with dark wooden blinds) the walls were lined floor to ceiling with books. It looked like the "arrangement" began in the far right corner of the room. The first volume there was white. While the other books varied in thickness they were all of uniform height. And they seemed to follow the color spectrum, more colors than Dump had ever imagined. Starting with that white book they darkened through every variant of every primary color until they reached a black book, located at the bottom of the wall facing them. The one with the windows that, had the blind been drawn up, would look out over the front yard.

Dump was eager to see what the book contained. Something nondescript like this was almost sure to contain pornography.

He opened it right up to the middle.

And was greatly disappointed. No gaping spread-legged poses. No emotionless couplings. Just a picture of a small block-like building, kind of gray in color, surrounded by a blue sky and resting on what looked like desert ground. Silently, he flipped through some more of the book. More of the same. Pictures of landscapes, sculptures, mountains, appliances. Every image seemed slightly familiar and slightly alien at the same time. Maybe it was just because, put in the context of a book, something bound between two covers and lovingly photographed, it made the ordinary seem like something else.

He glanced up at Leggy. Leggy had that angry look in his eyes. He shoved the book he had been leafing through up on a shelf and pulled out another one.

"What'd yours have in it?" Dump asked.

"Fuckin just pitchers of shit."

"Yeah, that's what mine is."

"This is gotta be some kinda joke or somethin."

"Maybe she's a photographer."

"Naw. Photographers got those special pitcher albums. Kinda like binders or somethin."

"Maybe she had these made special."

"Maybe she's just a crazy old cunt. Besides, some of these pitchers ain't right. I mean, you'd need some kinda Hollywood effects for some of this shit. Look here..." Leggy crossed the room with a couple strides of his long legs and showed Dump a picture in one of the books, this one a light purple color.

The book showed a tree but it was all wrong. The roots were

scraping at the sky and the leaves were down at the bottom. Another one showed some kind of flying device he had never seen before. It looked like one of those old round metal trashcans turned on its side with giant, papery moth wings.

"See," Leggy said. "Don't make no sense."

"Maybe it makes sense to Miss Blanchette."

"I tell you what: these books make me mad." Leggy put the book back on the shelf and took a quick swig from his flask. "But I'm takin one anyway."

"I don't think that's such a good idea," Dump said.

"Why the fuck not?"

"Well, it's stealing, for one thing. And, besides, what would be the point? You can't read it. Don't think you could sell it."

"Maybe they're real rare. I bet I could get somebody to put it on the computer."

"I say we just put em back and get the hell out."

"I say we help ourselves."

Dump replaced his book on the shelf and Leggy put his hand on the black one.

"I wouldn't take that one," Dump said.

"Fuck not?"

"She'd stand more of a chance of missing the first one or the last one but half of these are so close in color they almost look the same." And it was true. If you stood far enough away, you probably wouldn't be able to tell they were individual volumes.

"Guess you're right." Leggy's hand bounced to his left and landed on an espresso brown one. "This one'll do." He slid the thin hardcover book into the front of his pants and pulled his shirt, two maids in dresses emblazoned above the left breast pocket, over it. "Ready?"

"As I'll ever be."

They collected their things and headed out to the truck, locking the door behind them and stowing the key on a narrow ledge running just under the roof of the porch. Dump glanced at his watch. Just now four o'clock. They were finished early and he guessed that made it an okay day. As always, they would fudge their timesheets, probably putting down that they were out at five, and that almost made up for losing out on the tip.

"You wanna come back to my place, hang out for a bit?" Leggy asked.

Dump didn't really want to do that. He was kind of mad at Leggy but the alternative was to go back to his crappy apartment and listen to the wild children on one side of him yell and scream and the wild newlyweds on the other side of him fight for a few hours and then fuck each other's brains out for about ten minutes before they started fighting again. At least, he figured, Leggy would have some booze.

"Sure," Dump said, rolling the window down on the old truck as they wound out of Ms. Blanchette's neighborhood.

Somehow, Leggy had managed to save enough money to buy a couple of acres out in the country. Of course, that took all of his savings and the only thing he could afford to put on the land was a trailer. A *used* trailer at that. But out so far from the town limits nobody really gave a damn how it looked. Leggy didn't mind a little rust. As long as the inside was dry in the rain and warm in the winter.

Once at the trailer, they left their cleaning supplies to go inside and start in on some grape Mad Dog and a case of Natty Light. Leggy had a big screen TV and a satellite hookup and Dump watched a baseball pre-game. The Reds were playing the Pirates and he thought to himself what a godawful boring sport baseball was. Leggy continued to occupy himself with the dark brown book.

Leggy, entering the first stages of drunkenness, had started to repeat himself. "This book makes me real mad."

"Why?" Dump said, polishing off the last of the Mad Dog and cracking open another beer, a happy haze finally starting in his brain.

"I dunno. I guess books just make me mad. I don't see no point in em."

"Yeah. I guess."

"I mean, when you go to school they always tell you how you should read read read... Well, I been outta school a long time and I can't see where readin benefits nobody. Too much like work. And this here book. I don't understand. I don't think it's one of them photography books cause their ain't no captions or credits or nothin."

All in all, Dump was getting pretty fucking tired of hearing about the book.

"If you hate it so much why you keep lookin at it?"

"Cause I don't get it. There must be somethin special about it."

"Why you say that?" Dump downed his beer in three large gulps. Leggy's trailer was kind of warm and he could tell his stink had busted open again.

"Cause she had it all locked up. Had all of em locked up."

"I guess. Not many people lock up books, do they?"

"None that I know of. Of course, most people I know only own the Bible."

"The bestselling book of all time."

"The biggest piece of shit of all of them."

"Ain't never read it."

"Christ. You stink to high heaven."

"Sorry."

"Let's go out to the dirt pile. Let this place air out some."

"Game's gettin ready to start."

"You hate baseball."

"Guess you're right about that."

Dump stood up from the raggedy brown chair he had chosen to pollute, a little wobbly at first. Leggy crossed the small trailer and went into the back. Dump figured he was just going to use the bathroom but when he came back into the living room he was carrying his shotgun.

"What's with the gun?" Dump asked.

"I'm gonna have me some fun with this book."

"Gonna shoot it?"

"Damn right I'm gonna shoot it."

"Cool." Dump no longer gave a damn about the moral implications of stealing something Ms. Blanchette undoubtedly treasured.

Together, Leggy carrying the book and the shotgun, Dump carrying the half empty case of beer, they went out to the dirt mound, which was pretty much just that – a big mound of dirt, about six feet high and fifteen feet long. Neither of them really knew why it was there and neither of them really cared. They both liked to come out and fire off Leggy's arsenal from time to time and the dirt mound made a most excellent backstop.

Leggy opened the book up and placed it into some loose dirt on the mound.

"I'll fire one and then you can fire one, kay?"

"Sure." Dump cracked open another beer. He was about ready to piss his pants and wished he had used the toilet before coming out.

Leggy counted off about twenty paces and smiled. Some of the wax had sweated out of his mustache and it drooped a little bit. "Fuckin book." He pulled the trigger and Dump watched as bits of paper flew up from the book as the buckshot ripped into it. Leggy yipped and raised the rifle up in the air. Score one for the illiterates, Dump thought, and then said, "My turn."

"Get it right in the middle and we'll split that fucker in half," Leggy said.

"I'll try." When Dump looked through the sight, he saw two books and decided to aim for the one on the left.

The deafening roar of the shotgun threatened to split his skull but the effect was satisfying. The book didn't come completely apart but a large hole had opened in the middle.

Dump handed the gun back to Leggy. "You gonna give it another go?"

Leggy was now so drunk he had to hold his left eye open. He chose to do this with the end of the gun while he patted himself down with his free hand. "Shit," he said. "I didn't bring no more shells."

Dump staggered up to the mound, pulling his penis out of his dirty jeans. Once he got within pissing distance, he let go with a stream of rancid urine. It soaked the pages of the book.

"Shit, man," Leggy said. "I can smell that all the way back here. Don't make me blow your dick off." He aimed the unloaded gun at Dump. It still made Dump nervous.

They took the rest of the beer and the gun into the trailer and waited for dark. Destroying the book seemed to have taken both of their minds off it. They watched the baseball game, drank more, and played some cards. Eventually, after all the beer was gone, Dump decided he wanted to go back to the apartment. The truck was a company truck both of them used to do most of their driving. As long as it showed back up at Leggy's house in the morning to pick him up, he didn't really care where it went.

Leggy had fallen into something like a stupor on the couch. Dump didn't know how but he knew Leggy would be just as well-coiffed and crazy-eyed at nine o'clock in the morning as he had been earlier. Dump would be dragging. He didn't like to get this drunk through the week, on work nights, but sometimes there just wasn't anything else to do.

As he walked toward the truck, something caught his eye. Movement. Over by the dirt mound. His first crazy thought was that fucking book had some kind of tracking device in it and now the police had come to claim it. He thought about just hightailing it to the truck and driving away as fast as possible but he was too drunk to follow what could be considered the path of reason.

Drawing closer to the dirt pile, he saw the book had fallen down off its little ledge of soil.

And it seemed to be crossing the ground on its own.

Dump stopped there. That was some freaky shit. If the book was crawling now, he didn't want to be anywhere near it.

Then he noticed the book wasn't moving on its own. It was... *attached* to a figure.

Dump's heart began a hard thud in his weighty chest.

He moved closer to the book. The reason he couldn't see the figure so well at first was because it was covered in blood.

Now he was maybe ten feet away. He didn't know if he should move any closer to the figure, mainly because of the sheer oddity of the situation. But what harm could it do? It seemed to be pulling itself along the ground. And he had to know who it was. Because if his suspicions were correct then he would have to seriously reevaluate his reality.

The figure let out a garbled wheeze.

Besides, Dump thought, moving closer, what if this person needs help? He couldn't just turn and leave them. He wouldn't do that to anyone.

Now he was only a couple of steps away, looking down at the shattered and bloody face of Ms. Blanchette. Her body was riddled with buckshot. She reached toward him. Dump thought of something like a nuclear bomb, opening up some other world, ripping everyone up, turning them all into a shadow of this mutilated Ms. Blanchette.

"You don't know what you've done," she said. "You have to stop him." Her head dropped down, nearly hitting the grass.

"Stop who?" Dump asked.

"*Him.*"

"I think maybe I need to get you to a hospital." He said this knowing that a hospital wouldn't do any good. No doctor was good enough to patch up all those holes. And how would he explain this to the hospital staff? True, maybe they had shot her but she was a *book* when they shot her. Just a fucking book.

"Close it," she coughed up at him, dying madness in her eyes. "Please, let me die at home. Close it."

Dump reached down, the hole was opened as far as it could be. He didn't see how it was possible, didn't know how she would fit in the book, but he closed it anyway. And Ms. Blanchette was gone. He held the book in his right hand, not minding that there wasn't much of it to hold or that he had urinated on it only a couple of hours ago. It deserved better than to just be buried in a pile of dirt. Standing there, he realized he could very well be holding some kind of apocalypse.

He started back toward the trailer. He would have to wake Leggy up and tell him about this. He didn't know how he would take it. Since he hadn't actually *seen* Ms. Blanchette, half-in and half-out of the book, he probably wouldn't believe him at all.

Dump opened the door to the trailer.

Leggy was not at all how he had left him.

He was changed.

His legs were still very long but he had more of them. They bent from his torso, all six of them, like the fattest spider legs Dump had ever seen. His eyes had changed. They were silvery and slanted, reaching back nearly to his ears. And now his handlebar mustache was curved downward and looked more like fangs.

In front of him was the black book. The bastard had taken it after all. Had probably, in fact, known about the import of those books far longer than he had let on. For all Dump knew – and judging by what he now witnessed – Leggy wasn't human at all.

Briefly, watching this weird spiderthing in front of him, Dump thought back over all the years he had known Leggy. Curiously, he found himself thinking about all the stuff Leggy *hadn't* told him. He could spout philosophies, ideas, and opinions but he never talked about the good old days, the school days, the teenage years – the things most of their blue collar ilk talked about.

"Leggy," Dump said. He wished he had his gun. He wouldn't hesitate to put some bullets into this snarling thing in front of him.

Leggy didn't seem to hear Dump. He looked at the open book beneath him and Dump's eyes strayed in the same direction. The picture there was spread across two pages and looked very dark. Dump thought he saw other things, things like Leggy and some maybe even worse, flit across the pages. Leggy lowered his head and began squirming into the book. Shocked, Dump looked on, not knowing what else to do. He dropped the book he held in his hand onto the couch, picked up the shotgun that had been drunkenly tossed aside and went toward the back of the trailer.

In Leggy's bedroom was a strange smell. One Dump did not like at all. It was far worse than Dump usually smelled, even on his worst day. And there were pictures plastered on all the walls. Alien pictures. Pictures of things Dump could easily imagine existing in the pages of Ms. Blanchette's library. For all Dump knew, these pictures could have come from the books *in* Ms. Blanchette's library.

Dump rummaged through drawers until he found what he was looking for. The bright red plastic shells. He split the gun and put in two shells, heading back to the living room. Just as he entered, he saw the last of Leggy, heading into the black book, a toothed tail dragging along the worn down carpet.

Dump didn't hesitate. Maybe he had had enough of this world. Maybe he just couldn't stand the thought of that spider creature being loosed on some other world. Maybe it was the guilt at having aided in the theft and destruction of the other book. Maybe he had always hated Leggy. Picking up that other book and holding it in his free hand, Dump jumped into the black book after Leggy, having no idea what he would find on the other side.

13

Music from the Slaughterhouse

The midday sun continued to burn the already brown grass in the meadow. It was the hottest, driest summer Jakob could remember. Marcie, his younger sister by two years, sat next to him under a shady crabapple tree. Together, they stared across the field at the slaughterhouse. It was owned by their neighbor, Sully Bussard. Any breeze blown from the direction of the slaughterhouse was tainted. Especially in this heat. It smelled like meat gone bad and made Jakob think about what happened in there. Maybe it was a blessing that, today, the breeze was nonexistent.

"I don't like that place much," Marcie said.

"Me neither," Jakob said.

Marcie had brought her sketchpad out. She had completed her first year of high school where she had taken an art class and been absolutely consumed with her drawings and painting ever since. She sketched quickly with her left hand, holding the big sketchpad in her smaller right hand. Jakob didn't think anything of that hand's size deficiency until she actively used it. It looked strange. He tried to think of the word... *Anomaly*. That was the word he was thinking of. The hand looked totally out of place. It was the hand of a six-year-old girl.

"That's a good drawing," he said.

"Thanks."

He had almost forgotten why he had come out here. Then he remembered. Marcie's friend, Geneva Kaufman. He wanted to try and get Marcie to see if she liked him. He was seventeen and desperate and didn't see anything wrong with using his sister as a pimp.

He started to ask her about Geneva when a round of bleating came from the low white cinderblock slaughterhouse.

"Grotesque," Marcie mumbled under her breath.

"At least we don't get the smell today."

"Do you remember what dad used to tell us about the slaughterhouse, when we were too little to know it was a slaughterhouse?"

"Yeah. He said they made music in there and the sound of the cows dying was just some new music that wasn't played on the radios or anything yet. He said it sounded like it came from a whole other land."

"Yeah. It kind of made me want to go, like, look around in it or something. Only, when I got a little bit older and I knew what slaughterhouse meant I imagined they still played music in there only they used the ribs for a washboard, the eyeballs for castanets, and a bloated stomach as the drum."

"Jesus. That's sick, Marcie."

"Well, I wouldn't have thought all that stuff if Dad didn't fill our heads with that music nonsense."

"So it's his fault you're morbid?"

"Isn't it always the father's fault? Or the mother's? Maybe both."

She sat the notebook down in her lap and wiped some sweat away from her forehead with the small hand. Jakob was going to ask her about Geneva again but he remembered something he and his friend, Jeff, had seen the other night.

"Do you know if old Bussard's taken up with Darla Minnow?"

"Who?"

"Darla Minnow. The really fat librarian. You know... the one who's like so fat she has to use canes to walk?"

"No. Why?"

"I was just wondering. The other night when me and Jeff were out here we saw her wandering into the slaughterhouse. Well, I wouldn't really call it wandering. It was more like trundling."

"That's mean."

"I know. But why would she be there? Why would she be going into the slaughterhouse?"

"So how much had you and Jeff smoked while you were out here?"

Jakob stood up. "That's none of your business," he said. "Besides, you know we don't do that."

"Well, all I'm saying is you would have to be high not to notice the sort of obvious facts you've overlooked."

"Oh, well, I'm sure you'll fill me in."

"Okay. First, it's a slaughterhouse. They slaughter cows and other assorted animals so they can sell them for food. Sometimes, people provide the animal. They don't all come from Bussard's backyard. And if someone supplies an animal to be slaughtered then it only stands to reason they would have to come back to collect said animal. And, since our lady Minnow is of an expansive proportion, it would only stand to reason that she likes to eat. Maybe she lives on a farm. Maybe she had one of her animals slaughtered so she can rest easy knowing she has like a year's worth of hamburgers."

"Yeah. I guess. It just seemed kind of late."

"It's probably not like either of them had anything else to do."

"It's hot. I'm going inside. Oh, by the way, you know your friend Geneva...?"

"I knew there was a reason you were out here."

A few days later, Jakob lay in his bed in a post-masturbatory near-slumber when someone knocked on his bedroom door. He hurriedly zipped himself up and threw the soiled paper towel under the bed before saying, "Enter."

He propped himself up against the headboard. Marcie came in and sat on the far side of the bed.

"Why are you all sweaty?" she asked.

"Because it's hot."

"Oh, okay."

He didn't know why she had come in but she had a look of excitement in her eyes. Maybe she had finally asked Geneva about him. But she just sat there. She liked to do things like that. Like make him practically beg to get anything out of her.

"So why are you here?" he asked.

"Well... remember what you said about Darla Minnow the other day?"

"Yeah. And I also remember how you debunked my small town-really-creepy-love-affair theory."

"Maybe I was a bit hasty. You're not going to believe this."

Then she did it again. Just sat there on the edge of the bed with her lopsided hands clasped together, staring at him, waiting for him to ask her what it was he wasn't going to believe.

"*And?*" he said.

"Okay, so I just came back from the library. They have this really great Hieronymus Bosch book I was going to try and steal and Darla Minnow was there behind the counter only at first I didn't know it was her."

She stopped again.

"Okay," Jakob said. "If you keep making me pull the story out of you then I'm going to be too tired to pay attention by the time you're actually finished."

"I *could* just stop."

"No. Don't stop. Okay, *why* didn't you know it was her?"

"When she went into the slaughterhouse the other day, was she fat?"

"Of course she was fat. I don't know that I would have known it was her but for the girth and the canes."

"You are *so* mean. Anyway, the Darla Minnow I saw at the library was not fat. In fact, she was very thin. Like model-thin. I had a stroke of conscientiousness brought on by my curiosity and decided to check the book out instead of stealing it outright so I took it up to the counter and she got up from behind her desk to come and help me..."

"Did she have the canes?"

"No. No canes at all. She looked more like someone you would see dressed up as like the 'dirty librarian' in a *Playboy* spread or something."

"How's that possible?"

"That's what I've been wondering. You want to know what I

think?"

"You're the brain."

"I think something happened to her at the slaughterhouse."

"That's not possible." But Jakob was already turning the possibilities over in his head.

"We should watch it tonight. See if anybody goes in. And see what they look like when they come out."

"I don't know. It just sounds crazy. I'll call Jeff and see what he thinks."

"Well, I'm going to keep an eye on it and you can listen to your stupid friends if you want to. By the way, Geneva said you don't really have a chance. And she has a jealous boyfriend who may try and emasculate you if he sees you in public. I'm sure it's all talk but... well, he *is* pretty big."

"Talking to you makes my head hurt," Jakob said and reached for a music magazine on his bedside table, officially ending their conversation.

When she left, he picked up the cordless phone and called Jeff, hoping Jeff would be able to refute everything Marcie had told him. Instead, Jeff only agreed with her.

Jeff worked a part-time job at Bang's supermarket. He said the manager of Bang's was an older man with a limp. Until yesterday. Yesterday, he had come in looking twenty years younger without any trace of a limp. Jeff kept waiting for someone to ask about this sudden appearance change but the only thing anyone said was, "You're looking good today, Mr. Castle." Today, Jeff said, Mr. Castle had given Cynthia Raymond a "ride home," but Jeff suspected something much more prurient was at play.

"So," Jakob said, "you want to come and scout this place with me and my sister tonight?"

Jeff agreed, called Jakob a "gentleman and a scholar," and hung up.

Disappointment washed the night. By two o'clock, Jakob was tired of being bitten by mosquitoes and he was ready for bed. The two boys' sophomoric banter had frustrated Marcie about an hour ago and she had since retreated to the house.

"So, we done for the night?" Jeff asked.

"Yeah. I think so. This was stupid."

"Not if you saw Mr. Castle."

"That's supposing he came here. We don't know that he did."

"Still, people don't just transform overnight. Even if they have some kind of surgery, they have to have some healing time."

"I guess. Maybe we could just go to the library and ask Minnow about it tomorrow."

Jeff laughed. "Why? You just want to check her out?"

"Hardly."

"I hear she's pretty hot."

They walked through the meadow, swatting at mosquitoes and gnats, the sound of peepers and cicadas providing a churning whir in the background.

"You know," Jeff said. "Marcie'd be pretty hot if it wasn't for her hand."

"That's my *sister*. Besides, the hand's not so bad. I can imagine a pedophile taking a keen interest in her."

"God, you're sick."

When they got up to the house Jakob asked Jeff if he was staying tonight.

"No. I can't. I have to get up early and go to Bang's. Maybe I'll try and buddy up to Mr. Castle. See if I can get some kind of confession from him."

"Meet back here tomorrow?"

"Sure."

Jakob went back into the house and went to bed. Lying there, he thought about the slaughterhouse. The place had always unnerved him but he found himself now terrified of it. He didn't know why exactly. If it was making people "beautiful" that should be a lot less terrifying than thinking of the slaughters it was normally used for. But he didn't like the idea. In his German class, they had discussed Faust, and it seemed like there had to be something Faustian about this. One does not get something for nothing. Then he had another horrifying thought. The thought actually came to him in Jeff's voice. It was what he had said when they were walking back from the field, "Marcie'd be pretty hot if it wasn't for her hand."

No, Jakob thought. Marcie wouldn't even think about that. He knew she wasn't a shallow person and he thought she had actually grown quite comfortable with the idea of her hand over time. If she had asked he could have told her the hands were like the *last* things guys looked at.

He couldn't get the idea out of his head.

Maybe it wouldn't hurt to get up and check on her. Act big brotherly for a change. He was the one who had brought the whole thing up to begin with. If something happened to her, he would be partially to blame. He didn't want the guilt.

The wooden floor in his room squeaked as he walked across it. He opened his door and looked down the hall. Her room was at the end of the hall and he saw that her light was still on. Maybe she fell asleep with it on. She was never up this late and she had seemed pretty tired at the stakeout. He walked down the hall and gently knocked on the door. He didn't hear any answer and just assumed she was asleep but decided to open the door and check on her anyway.

When he opened the door she wasn't in her bed.

He looked at the walls of her room, all of her drawings and paintings hung up with masking tape as though she were still deciding which ones to keep there. Dominating the wall above her bed was a painting that did not alleviate his paranoid thoughts at all. It was on an open-hardback size canvas. There was something childlike about it. It looked like she had dipped her hands in paint—the left one in primary green and the right one, the small one, in primary red—and pressed them to the canvas. Scrawled all around the colorful hands in black ink were the words: MY SCHIZOPHRENIC HANDS. Over and over.

Jakob ran out of his house and out to the meadow. Maybe he could still catch her before it was too late.

The night was a buzzing swarm, matching some internal rant raging within Jakob. He reached the rusted fence separating his property from Old Man Bussard's and clumsily made his way over the top. A dim light glowed from inside the slaughterhouse. Jakob didn't want to go in. He had never been this close to it. He didn't like it.

It made his skin crawl. He slapped at a gnat that had kamikazed into his forehead.

And now he was going to go inside the slaughterhouse.

His stomach did a great turn. The smell increased as he drew closer. Standing at the rusted iron door between him and the mystery waiting inside, he wanted to be able to tell himself this was crazy so he could go back home and curl up in his bed, surrounded by air conditioning and a lack of insects. But Marcie might be in there.

No, he told himself. Marcie *had* to be in there. Where else would she be? He couldn't believe he hadn't seen the signs earlier. She had never been interested in creepy things like the slaughterhouse before. Then, after being presented with the alluring prospect of self-transformation, she had suddenly wanted to find an answer to all the mysteries.

Jakob grabbed the handle of the door and yanked it to his left. It slid into place with a clanking boom. The smell hit him, threatening to drop him to his knees. It was the worst thing he had ever smelled. Occasionally, a raccoon would get smashed on the road in front of the house and rot there for a few days until the park ranger removed it. That was enough of a deathsmell for Jakob. This was a hundred times worse. This smelled like what he imagined burying his nose in the roadkill raccoon might be like.

His stomach tried to bolt up his spine but he managed to hold it down.

He looked frantically for Marcie but didn't see her.

He didn't see anything.

Of course not. He had himself all worked up over nothing. This was, after all, just a slaughterhouse. Crazy old Bussard had probably just left the light on accidentally. Whatever he had seen previously was probably not what he thought he had seen. Maybe Ms. Minnow *had* lost a bunch of weight and maybe the person he had seen entering the slaughterhouse the one night wasn't Ms. Minnow. He doubted everything now. Maybe Jeff had made up the whole Mr. Castle scenario. Jeff had been known to tell wild stories until everyone believed him before telling his audience it was a lie.

"Marcie?" he called out, just to be sure.

No one answered him.

Okay, he had served his big brotherly duty. Now he just wanted to get out. He turned around and saw Bussard standing in the doorway.

"Lookin for somethin?" Mr. Bussard said.

"No. I was just leaving. I'm sorry. I thought my sister was in here." Surely the old man would understand that. He looked perfectly reasonable, just like he had always looked – a short man with bandy legs and a big gray mustache.

"You two playin games or somethin?"

"Yeah. Something like that. It was stupid of me to look for her in here. I'm gonna go now. Sorry if I bothered you."

Bussard stepped aside to allow Jakob passage to the outside.

"You kids get stranger every day," Bussard said. "Hidin out in a slaughterhouse." He laughed a gentle laugh. "I'll let it pass this time but you can see how it concerns me. You bein out here. Some people might wanna steal my cattle and I can't have that." Bussard stepped farther into the slaughterhouse and motioned Jakob out the door, a look something like interested disappointment on his face.

"I understand. Good night." Jakob stepped through the threshold and lost his footing. Falling forward he caught himself with his elbows. Clumsy idiot, he thought. I can't even walk away gracefully. He tried to stand up and fear seized his heart. His feet were drawn together. Bussard was dragging him into the slaughterhouse.

"You noticed all the beautiful people in town?" Bussard said.

"Let me go," Jakob said, his mouth dry, panic taking over. He struggled to scoot away but it was useless. The chain bit into his ankles and Bussard looped one of the links onto a hook.

It was some kind of pulley system. He turned a little lever about ten feet from Jakob and Jakob felt himself rising up from the ground, suspended by his feet. Jakob screamed. He screamed for Marcie. He screamed for his mom and dad.

"You can scream all you want," Bussard said. "The only thing anybody ever hears is music. Or a cow. They make what they want to out of it, I guess."

"There's nothing wrong with me!" Jakob spat. "I don't want you to change anything."

"But everybody wants something to change. Sure, you don't have any major flaws but if you looked *even better* you probably wouldn't have any problems at all."

"Let me go!" Jakob shouted, flailing his arms wildly, trying to swing on the chain and get close enough to Bussard to do some harm.

"Besides," he said, grabbing a sledgehammer leaning against the dark stained wall. "It's not so much about changin anything. It's more about dyin. And bein reborn. And me ownin a little piece of you that was all yours once upon a time."

Jakob took a deep breath, ready to scream again, before the hammer smashed into his face and everything he had ever known about life was sent spiraling into some black space.

Marcie came up from the basement. That was where the big TV was and, when she had returned to the house after the stakeout, she realized she wasn't as tired as she thought. She walked past Jakob's room and noticed his door was open. She had to admire his and Jeff's tenacity. They were really taking this seriously. Marcie was now so tired she could hardly hold her eyes open. She didn't know how Jakob was still awake. She shut the door to her bedroom, turned off the light, and crawled into bed. As she lay there in silence, she thought she heard the music from the slaughterhouse and laughed it off. She really had become obsessed over the past couple of days. It was stupid, really, she figured. Just before she submitted entirely to sleep she had a strange notion. She wished she hadn't told Jakob Geneva had said those things about him. Genny hadn't even really said that. She had actually said she thought he was pretty cute but Marcie had wanted to have fun with him. What if Jakob had gone into the slaughterhouse, seeking the same thing that Mr. Castle and Ms. Minnow had sought? All so Geneva would find him more attractive. She drifted off to sleep, convincing herself the noise she heard was just a conglomeration of the country night sounds and her speculations about Jakob were just the product of her somewhat warped creative mind.

A Butterfly in Ice

1.

"Joel."

The voice came from very far away, swimming toward him.

"Jooooel?"

The voice was unrecognizable.

Joel Vernon struggled to open his sandy eyes. Scraping open, he had the feeling they had been closed for a very long time. He stared into blackness.

No. It wasn't blackness. It was...

Pupils.

"Good," the man who owned the pupils said softly, pulling his face away from Joel's. "You're awake."

Joel resisted the urge to speak. Didn't even know if he could. He resisted the urge to ask the man in front of him a million questions. Already, a frantic feeling of dislocation rolled around in his brain. He sensed rather than felt his eyes darting around the room. A room unlike any other he had ever seen and the man in front of him was unlike any other man he had ever seen.

The man's black pupils, set in irises just as dark, were the only breaks in the monotonous white of this room. Even the rest of the *man* seemed to be white. His hair was white, even though the taut skin of his face suggested he was not old enough to have a head of totally white hair. His skin was very pale and not reddish pale but powder white vampire pale. He wore a white outfit Joel immediately thought of as a uniform. A name was embroidered into the chest of the uniform's shirt, right over the heart, and Joel didn't know if it was the man's name or some kind of logo. The embroidery was white. It said: SNOW. So this man in front of him was potentially "Mr. Snow," Joel thought. He couldn't think of a more appropriate name for this man to have.

Joel scanned the entire room. There wasn't really anything to take in. It was like trying to take a drink from an empty cup.

Everything was white.

White walls. White door. White floor. White ceiling. White bedside table. White chair in the corner. White blinds covering a window. After spotting those blinds, Joel wondered what would happen if he lifted them. Would everything outside be white, also?

This made him wonder how long he had been here, wherever *here* was.

"How long have I been here?" Joel asked, not really knowing why he put this before the other obvious questions like "Where am I?" and "Who are you?"

Snow looked at Joel with an expression he couldn't quite place. He didn't think there was caring in those eyes. Neither did there seem to be any malice. Sadness, maybe.

"You've been resting here for some time, Joel," Snow said, his voice low and soothing.

"Where am I?"

"Well, that's difficult to explain. You're in a hospital of sorts."

"Of sorts? Which hospital?"

"You need to rest, Joel. *Rest.*"

So maybe this man, Snow, was a doctor. Dr. Snow. Apparently, Snow noticed the wildness in Joel's eyes. He held up a small sky blue pill in front of his face.

"Here," he said. "This will help you rest." And then he placed it into Joel's mouth. His fingers, while gloveless, tasted of latex.

Something inside Joel revolted. He didn't want to swallow the pill. He didn't want to swallow anything this man was going to give him.

Snow rose from the bed to his full height. From Joel's position on the bed, Snow seemed very tall.

"I'll return shortly," Snow said, leaving the room.

Joel raised his hands up to pull the pill from his mouth and noticed he had no hands. The sleeves of his thick white shirt descended past his hands, where they were sewn tightly shut. Quickly, before the pill dissolved, he turned his head and spit it onto the floor.

Bad idea, he thought. The semi-dissolved pill made a small bright blue splash on the harsh white of the floor. Sliding out of the bed, he attempted to stand up, his rubbery legs immediately dumping him back on the floor. Panic seized him. What the hell was he going to do with the pill? He took another quick scan of the room, searching for a bathroom door. Surely there had to be a bathroom in here and if there was then he could just take the pill in there and flush it down the toilet.

For a few frustrating seconds, he tried to pick up the pill, succeeding only in making a bigger mess. The blue was all over his elongated sleeve. How could something as small as that pill make such a big mess? Finally managing to pick up the pill, he stood, contemplating where he could put it.

No. There didn't seem to be any bathroom doors in the room. None at all. This worried him on a whole other level but the only thing he could think about for the moment was getting rid of that funny blue pill. He looked toward the window. Deep down, he knew it wouldn't open but he decided he had to try. He crossed the room to the window and pulled on the white cord he thought would lift the blinds. They didn't budge. He reached under the blinds, thinking maybe he could pull them out a little but they seemed to be fastened to the wall. Now he was as thirsty for a glimpse outside as he was to find a place to stash the pill. He attempted to pry a couple of the slats apart so he could look out of the window but there weren't any spaces in between them. They were like very convincing faux blinds. Like they were just carved out of the wall or something. He doubted there was even a window behind those blinds.

Snow said he would be coming back but he did not say when he would be coming back and there was still the matter of hiding the pill and then trying to get the stain off the floor, knowing it would just end up on his sleeve.

He took a firm grip on the pill. He had an idea of what he could do with it. He slid his covered hand down the back of his pants. Before he could really think about what he was doing, he pushed the blue pill between his buttocks and into his anus just far enough for the sphincter muscles to close around it. When he pulled his hand back up there was some brown now mixed with the blue on his shirt.

More like a straitjacket, he thought. Why the hell would they need to put me in some kind of straitjacket? Why am I even here? Do they think I'm some kind of danger to myself?

With the pill safely hidden away, he crouched down on the floor and spit at the blue spot, vigorously wiping it with his sleeve and wondering how he had arrived here. And for the first time since being conscious he was gripped with a single emotion.

Fear.

True and pure, it dripped ice down his spinal column.

It rattled his bones as he climbed back into bed, grateful to give his wobbly legs a rest.

2.

Maria Pearl. That was who he thought of when he went to sleep. Maybe it was more than thinking of her. Maybe it was dreaming her because here, in his dream, he wasn't sure she had ever existed. He saw her laughing face, green eyes winking out of sunsplashed red cheeks, orange hair flaming crazily away from her head like the sun's corona.

She was a dream... maybe. If he had ever had her, he couldn't imagine letting her go and if he had not had her, then he realized his life still had a purpose.

She wasn't the only thing in the dream. There was a whole other place there. A summer place. Joel heard the shrieking of the insects, reveled in the sight of the swollen green trees. A stream trickled lazily in the distance.

Suddenly, Maria's smile faded. She looked at him and said, "We have to go. I think there's someone else here."

And, just like that, the dream was gone.

3.

He woke up, shivering, searching the room. How could he have let himself fall asleep? Did he even remember being awake? Was that the first time he had been awake?

Snow stood over by the window. The blinds were now open, pulled all the way to the top of the window frame, and Joel wondered how this could be since, only a little while before, he had found the blinds to be completely impenetrable. As if sensing he was awake, Snow turned toward him, approaching the bed, moving slowly and languidly, those black eyes swimming in a sea of white.

"You're awake," he said.

"I have questions." Joel didn't know how he was going to force those questions out, didn't know if he was going to be *able* to force those questions out when it seemed impossible to make his brain form words.

"We *all* have questions. I don't expect you to answer any of *my* questions."

Joel didn't know what to say to that but he couldn't just lie back in the bed. He couldn't just lie there and not do anything. He didn't know why he was here. He didn't know if he should even be here. He didn't know where here was. But he didn't know if this man, Snow, was to blame. Joel's first instinct was to attack him. To get past him somehow... but what if Snow was there to help him?

Snow rubbed his powdery hands together. "Actually," he said. "I do have one question you could answer for me... At least, I think you can answer it. Stand up." Snow, now bedside, reached down and helped Joel out of the bed. Joel stood up, his legs a little less shaky. Maybe, he thought, that was because he didn't take the pill. The pill *this man* had given him.

"Let's come over to the window," Snow said, cradling Joel's elbow and leading him. The only thing Joel could see from where he stood was a vast expanse of blue sky. "There's someone I would like you to identify for me."

Joel stood at the window. His eyes widened. He didn't see whoever it was Snow was talking about. The only thing he could see was that it was summer. Joel didn't know why that knowledge aroused such emotion within him but, just standing out there and looking at the foliage beyond the window, the bright flowers in bloom, the trees growing mammoth past the parklike ocean of green, blowing lazily in a sultry breeze, made him want to shatter the window to be out there in all of that sun and warmth. To be out there in that climate that was the complete antithesis of the climate currently enveloping him.

"You're looking off in the distance. Look down. Down there on that bench. Do you see that girl?"

Joel saw her and, as impossible as it seemed, his eyes widened further.

4.

The first time Joel saw Maria Pearl was in a summer sculpture class at Gethsemane College. It was a sprint class, mostly intended for people who needed a few credits in order to graduate on time. The class met three times a week at four hours a meeting. Joel had taken his customary seat on a bench in the back corner of the room. Maria was a good fifteen minutes late. There was a universal pause as she walked into the classroom, made her apologies to the professor and came to the back of the class, taking up the empty bench next to Joel.

He found himself staring at her all through the class. They were stolen stares, sure, nothing too open, but he found himself glancing at her every few seconds. Red hair. Green eyes. Pale skin flushed red. A baggy t-shirt. Baggy blue jeans, cut low enough so Joel could tell she wore black underwear. The underwear contrasted with the paleness of her skin. He felt like an ogling pervert and realized he didn't care. He was shy by nature, had never approached a girl before in his life but he determined, from first laying eyes on Maria, that he was going to attempt to get her to go out with him.

Turns out it wasn't as hard as he thought.

After the class was over, she stood up from her bench, arms dusty up to the elbows with dried clay, and looked at Joel. Maybe she sensed some desperate, urgent longing in his stare.

"I'm Maria," she said. She pulled an odd-looking sculpture from her canvas bag so she could put her sculpting tools in it.

"I'm Joel. That's cool," he said, pointing to the sculpture.

"Thanks," she said. "It's called 'A Butterfly in Ice.'"

"Cool name." Jesus, he felt like a putz. "So I haven't seen you around campus. Are you new?"

"Kind of. My parents moved here from Arizona. Dad's with the Air Force. We moved too late for me to enroll in the last semester so I have to do the summer thing."

"Welcome to Ohio," Joel said, feeling stupid. He was still marveling at the fact this mysterious girl now seemed so down to earth, with parents and everything. It seemed foreign to her.

"What do you people do for fun out here," she asked, pulling her heavy backpack off the floor and slinging it over her shoulder. It pulled her shirt tight against her breasts. She picked up her sculpture and, watching the muscles in her forearm flex, Joel noticed the sculpture *did* look like a butterfly trapped in ice, in an abstract kind of way.

"This is the Midwest, we don't have fun," Joel said.

She laughed briefly. Joel's insides melted.

"Right... but I thought you like watched racecars and farmed and shot guns and stuff like that."

"Well, maybe I'm not the best person to ask about recreation."

"Why not?"

"Not many friends. I don't really do much. Study. Read. Study."

"Well, you have another friend now... what was your name again?"

He coughed, ready to tell her his name when she put a hand on his chest, stopping him.

"I know," she said. "It's Joel. I was just kidding."

She drew her hand from his chest, kind of sliding it downward as she did and asked if he wanted to do something this weekend.

"I'd love to."

And then they went their separate ways. At the close of the next class, they made plans to go out on Friday after class.

The rest of the week was interminable. The class ended in the afternoon and they went to a bar close to the campus. They were both kind of drunk and decided the bar was too full for them. They went to a park and sat in a pair of swings, the empty park somewhat spectral in the moonlight and Maria told him she had never seen the ocean. Joel, whose family made regular trips to Florida, told her they would have to change all that. They ended up in his car, racing east on the highway. Sometime the next day they were in North Carolina at a nearly deserted expanse of beach.

"Well, here we are," Joel said, as though they had taken a quick trip around the block.

The weather couldn't have been more perfect. The sky was blotted with far away puffs of clouds. They ran along the beach all day, the water warm, splashing up around them, the sun baking them. There was a lot of laughter. Joel couldn't remember laughing like that since he had been a kid. He couldn't remember feeling that unabashedly *good* since he had been a kid. And it wasn't just his lust for Maria making him feel that way. They had not done so much as hold hands at that point.

They stayed on the beach until sunset. Once the sun was out of sight, they retreated up to his car in the deserted parking lot.

"Maybe we should rest before driving back," she said.

He couldn't argue with her, having been up well over twenty-four hours. They both crawled in the backseat of the car and there they kissed for the first time. To Joel, that was what made the whole day a dream. Those innumerable seconds with his lips pressed against hers assured him he would be able to remember the day in shimmering glimpses at best. It was this he would remember in its entirety. He fought the urge to let his hands explore her. He didn't want her to feel like she had to let him just because he had driven all this way and was her only real way back.

"Now, was that fun?" she asked.

"Yes," Joel said. "That was fun."

They fell asleep in the backseat, Maria's head resting against his shoulder, the wild fragrance of her hair there to stimulate even his sleeping mind.

They awoke just before dawn, climbing out of the car to stretch and move into the front seat. In this meager blue-gray light, the beach now seemed sullen and cold, summer faded in a night. An old man walked slowly along the beach, casting awkward glimpses at the car.

The trip back was not nearly long enough for Joel. They talked about books and music and movies, told stories from their childhoods, lived nearly a continent apart but with eerie similarity.

5.

"Familiar, huh?" Snow said, his breath icy on the back of Joel's neck.

"What the fuck is going on?" Joel said. "I want to talk to her."

"Why? She wouldn't know who you are. That's not who you think it is. That's her twin sister."

"She didn't have a twin sister."

"How well do you think you really knew her?"

"What is this? Is this some kind of game?"

"This is life, Joel. And you're making a mess of it. Not quite following orders. I can tell when you do not do as you're told. It's all over your sleeves. It's all over the floor. I want you to get back in the bed."

"And what if I don't want to get back into bed?"

"Then you will never know what happened. I have the answers. You have the questions. Who has the power?"

Joel didn't know what to think. He knew what he wanted to do. He wanted to tear through the glass in front of him. He wanted to float down on the summer breeze until he stood in front of that model of perfection sitting languidly on the parkbench. Maria didn't have any twin sisters. He would have known if she did. Even though he had never been invited back to her house (there hadn't been any time for that) he knew she would not have left out a detail such as that. Nevertheless, his mind raced. Part of him still wanted to believe what this man was telling him. That was the same part of him that wanted to believe Snow was there to help him.

"Get back in the bed, Joel... and I'll tell you a story."

Reluctantly, Joel pulled himself away from the window. What could he do, really? Would there be any escaping this man in his current weakened and doped-up state? He didn't think so. There wouldn't be any fighting. There could be little resistance of any kind. Even without Snow's suggestions, the only thing Joel really wanted to do was to get back into bed, curl up under the white blankets that afforded at least a modicum of warmth and listen to the air conditioning hum continuously from the vent overhead.

Joel climbed back in the bed, his muscles hungrily reaching for the mattress, wanting nothing more than to be immobile. Snow came and sat on the side of the bed, staring off across the room. He took a deep breath, preparing to tell Joel why he was here.

6.

The first time Joel had sex with Maria was like this:

It was the weekend after their beach excursion.

He had driven them to the nature reserve at dusk. He was pretty sure they both knew what it was they wanted. They found a clearing located deep enough in the woods for them to hide and spread a quilt out on the ground. He had stuck some incense into the soft earth around the quilt and lit it. Soon the air was redolent with the sweetness of summer and the perfumes of nag champa.

It didn't take them long. They greeted each other's bodies with near ferocity and, afterwards, they lay there in silence, smoking cigarettes and looking at the stars. She lay on her stomach, her legs bent so her feet dangled above her rounded ass. He stroked the two strange, nearly-identical scars on her back and fought the urge to ask her how she got them.

"This is our spot," she said out of nowhere.

"What?" he asked.

"This is our spot. The next time we do this, it has to be right here. For now. And then we can make more spots."

"Sticky spots," he said. He wrapped an arm around her shoulders and pulled her nakedness closer to him. There they kind of drifted off.

And awoke nearly an hour later to a rustling in the woods.

"What is that?" he asked, startled.

"Some kind of animal," she said.

"Then it's a fucking huge animal," he hissed under his breath. He figured it was more likely a park ranger and, gathering their clothes and the quilt, they both sprinted along the trail until they reached his car.

7.

"I'm surprised you don't remember what happened." Snow's voice was annoyingly calm. Devoid of any compassion whatsoever. "It was so tragic. But I guess some minds can simply erase tragedy. You've been here ever since."

"What happened?"

"You really don't remember, do you?"

"You promised."

"It was a terrible car crash. You were driving. You were a little more than drunk. Shouldn't have been driving. You swerved to avoid something in the road. Your car turned over and slid down a hill. You went into a coma. This morning was the first time you came out of that coma. Maria was killed. Not instantly. No, for a while, she was here with you. She died this morning. That is her sister out there, ready to go home, ready to begin preparations for the funeral. It's a short story really."

Joel didn't know what to think. His heart thudded sickeningly in his chest as he lay there. Why did he have any reason to doubt this man? What else would explain why he was here in a hospital?

"How long have I been here?" Joel asked.

"Three months."

"Why am I wearing a straitjacket?"

"It's not a straitjacket. Your hands are covered so you won't scrape out your eyes in your sleep. We've discovered some people who undergo violent trauma suffer very physical rages even while in a coma."

"Why is everything white?"

"Lack of stimulus."

"But you let me look outside."

"That was because I wanted you to feel like you were looking at Maria for one last time. Trying to trigger some memories. I shouldn't have done that. It's not in the rules."

"I'm glad you did."

"I need you to take this pill for me."

Snow placed the pill in his mouth just as he did last time. Then he stood to leave. This time, thinking he was some kind of murderer, Joel took the pill, let it slide down his throat, hoping it would quell some of the strong emotions that had risen within him.

8.

The next weekend and the next weekend and the one after that, they went to their secret place in the woods. There was always a sound to creep them out, always the thought of someone looming just outside the perimeter of the clearing, watching them, listening to them, consuming them. Maybe it was just some sick voyeur or maybe it was a park ranger or maybe it was some horrifically huge shaggy beast. Neither of them knew. Neither of them cared. They left fulfilled.

On their last night together, a stranger thing happened.

After their lovemaking, they lay in their customary position, Joel flat on his back, Maria curled up between his arm and torso. He saw something flutter just above them.

"What is that?" She had seen it too.

"I think it's a butterfly," he said. He reached up casually, not expecting to catch it. But it seemed like the butterfly wanted to be caught. At first, he had thought it was just one of those butterflies you see flapping through summer fields, the small white kind.

After bringing it down into his palm, he saw that it was different. It looked like it was covered in ice crystals.

"Oh, this is beautiful," Maria said and Joel could have sworn the butterfly turned toward her voice, acknowledging her in some way. "It's just like my sculpture."

"Touch it," he said. "It's cold."

She reached out a finger and stroked the back of the little white butterfly. "Feels like ice."

"Weird, huh?"

"Put your clothes on. Let's let it go and see where it lands."

He had realized she was able to make a game out of just about anything. He was usually willing to play along and he always enjoyed himself.

The night was strange. A clear full moon kind of night that

35

seemed way too bright. A night full of shadows that moved.

He put his clothes on, watching Maria slide into hers. He had always found this nearly as sensual as watching her slide out of her clothes. Once clothed, they chased after the strange icy night butterfly. And it was like the butterfly wanted them to follow it, the way it hovered there at the edge of the clearing, never letting itself escape their range of sight.

Beckoning, he thought. *It's like the butterfly is beckoning us.*

9.

Again, consciousness found him. Opening his eyes in the winter room, a sudden panic seized him. He had to get out of here. He had to get out and get as far away as possible because this place was not any good. Not any good at all. This place was a prison, an icy prison, and he knew the longer he stayed, the thicker and stronger the ice would freeze until he would not be able to even entertain any thoughts about escaping.

He melted from the bed. Some form of stored heat inflated his muscles, making him feel strong again. He didn't think his legs would give out anytime soon. He half expected Snow to be there in the room with him, there to shove him back in the bed and cram another pill down his throat, to ice the sweat beading on his forehead.

Joel ran to the door and pulled at it. Locked. Of course. This only reinforced the idea that this place was a cell.

He crossed the room until he reached the blinded window. How had Snow made the blinds go up? Joel ran his fingers around the edges, not finding so much as an opening. He wanted to scream but knew that would not do him any good. Screaming would only attract attention. He went back to the bed, pulling on it, sliding it out from the wall, thoughts of dismantling swarming his brain. Memories trickled from his thawing thoughts. Memories, he knew, that were the correct memories. Even though they were not as solid and resolute as the memories Snow had supplied for him, he knew they were the correct memories because they were *his*.

10.

Maria *hadn't* wanted to follow the butterfly. She chased him chasing the butterfly through the woods. They were not on one of the main trails. This trail was narrow and unmaintained. Hardly a trail at all.

Strange feelings tugged at Joel. This was the first time he had ever felt badly when in the presence of Maria. They jogged down a slight hill and the thought, more like a warning, popped up in his brain... and she just kept yelling at him to stop.

Something bad was going to happen.

And looking ahead in the oddly luminous night, he noticed the woods didn't look right. He wanted to heed her warnings but he couldn't stop.

The woods ahead of them were melting.

No longer individual rigid structures, the trees and shrubs became something like richly colored water. All the daytime green, painted purple in the night, slowly ran down the canvas of the horizon. Peeking through was something that looked like ice.

The butterfly swam through the air as if desperate for this new, surreal landscape. Joel watched it disappear into the waterfall of the woods and staggered backward with a blinding light and shocking force. Like a block of ice hitting him in the chest.

11.

Try as he might, Joel was not able to dismantle the bed. It was like the whole structure was made from a single piece of metal. That meant he would have to use the bed itself as a weapon. He squeezed in behind the head of the bed and waited, readying himself, his muscles tense.

He didn't know how long he waited for Snow. He was about ready to give up. There was probably a camera set up somewhere, watching his every move. He didn't have much faith Snow was going to open the door and walk into the trap Joel had laid for him. But he wouldn't give up there. He would give it a few more minutes and if Snow had still not come back then Joel planned on going over to the window and pounding on that. He would use the bed if he had to. Rage made him strong. Rage made him burn.

Just when he was about ready to give up, Snow opened the door.

Joel drove the bed forward. The foot of the bed slammed into the doctor, knocking him into the far wall.

Now, however, the bed obstructed the doorway so Joel had to waste precious moments pulling the bed back into nearly the same position it was before. By the time he did that, Snow stood in the doorway, a gun in his hand. The gun was white, small and sinister-looking.

"Stop," Snow said.

"I didn't think doctors carried guns."

"I didn't think patients tried to kill their doctors."

"You fed me lies before. Who are you?" If he was going to die at the end of this man's gun then he felt he at least had the right to know why it was he was dying.

"You've seen me before. I'm surprised you were so shocked to see me here... in my home."

"What do you mean I've seen you before?"

"And I've seen you. I've watched you for a long time. Actually, that's not true. I've watched Maria for a long time. And then you came along. Did you ever feel like you were never alone?"

"You were the one." Joel should have seen this before. The shivers in the bushes. The man on the beach who had only been mistaken as elderly. This man was Joel and Maria's collective unease.

"Do you know what it was like watching you take something I've wanted for so long?"

"You're sick."

"Yes, Joel. I'm glad you realize that. In fact, I don't think you know just how sick I am. Do you know how many times Maria has moved in the last ten years, ever since she turned twelve?"

"She moved around a lot."

"It's not because her dad was in the military. Everywhere she went, there was someone there, stalking her, making her feel like a victim... or at least a potential victim. The police were called a number of times but they could never find anything. Not as long as I had this place, all wrapped up in ice and hidden just slightly behind reality."

"But that's insane."

"Who's to say what's insane anymore? You're here, aren't you?"

"But why... why her?"

"Let's just say that I'm not fully human, Joel. I'm not a god. Nothing as glamorous as that. But I was close. An angel maybe. I wasn't always a bad person. I was given this home and the ability to change some things. To *influence* some things. But then I saw this girl one day. It was in Maine. I'll never forget it. She was in the lake and the undercurrent was pulling her down. I had the ability to become the undercurrent, to change it. And that was what I did. I became the undercurrent. I released her and she swam to safety. But I couldn't stop watching her. And it didn't stop there. Over the next several months, I couldn't take my eyes from her. Eventually, I was told I had to quit this voyeurism or risk losing my powers. It was an easy choice to make. But I didn't lose all of my powers. Only the ones that gave me any sense of self-worth. So I hope you understand what I am about to do. I hope you understand because I have sacrificed everything I once had to have Maria here, in the closest thing I have to a home. And you are not going to keep me from that."

Snow raised the gun and fired at Joel. Joel threw himself to the side, the bullet catching him in the left arm. A spray of red cascaded across the pristine winter room. Joel rolled toward Snow, knowing only that he wanted to be close enough to get him out of the way. Instead, he made himself an easier target. He looked up to the gun hovering only inches from his face.

And then he heard a loud sound.

Metal on bone. Bone or ice?

Joel saw the metal bar hit Snow's head. And he saw Snow's head erupt in a frosty shower like a shattered ice cube. And then Snow changed. He shrunk, becoming the butterfly that had led him to this place. Standing where he once stood was Maria.

She smiled down at him.

"Are you ready to get out of here?"

"What about him?"

"He's just a butterfly."

12.

Joel followed Maria out of the house, into the heat, into the summer. He held Maria in his arms, looking back the way they had come. On the floor of the forest was a large block of ice and, inside that block of ice, there was a frozen butterfly, its wings spread wide. He had to look hard to see it. It could have just as easily been a bubble in an ice cube. This, he realized, was Maria's sculpture.

"I'm still not sure I understand," Joel said.

"Well, that's because you never believed in angels."

"I'd never given it much thought."

"Snow was a foolish one. Self-righteous. Always thinking he was the only one being punished."

"What do you mean?"

"When an angel wants something that is human, they become human themselves, possessing only powers of destruction." Maria approached the block of ice and put her hands onto it. Joel watched as the block melted into a puddle, the butterfly wriggling in the middle of it, before the puddle burst into flame.

"Are you..." Joel started.

"You were eleven the first time I saw you. You were flying a kite in your backyard. I made myself an eleven-year-old girl, knowing one day we would meet. I hope that doesn't frighten you. Snow had no idea I had fallen from grace when he tried to save me. That was probably what attracted him to me... because I was so much like him."

Joel didn't know what to think. He was just glad to be alive. He was glad Maria was alive. Everything else would have to come after those two facts. There were so many questions.

"You're not going to freeze me in a block of ice?"

"No. I promise."

"Then I guess I'll have to be okay with that. How do you know *I'm* not an angel?"

She grabbed his hand and put it on her back. He rubbed the smooth scars between her shoulderblades.

"Because you don't have these."

The Spot

1.

"That was nice," Mary said.

Joe kissed the top of her head and reached over onto the nightstand for his cigarettes. Mary lay pressed against him, on her side, her left arm slung over his chest. Fortunately, Joe was able to fit a king-size bed into his apartment and they were able to gravitate toward one half of it in order to avoid the dreaded spot splashed across the other half. Tomorrow he would change the sheets. It would be the first time in a while he had had to do that.

Joe lit his cigarette and offered one to Mary. "No thank you," she said.

"Would you like me to turn on the TV?"

"I'm fine. I'm actually quite tired. I think I'll go."

"No, stay. You don't need to be out this late."

"Are you sure?"

"Certain."

Joe smoked his cigarette and wished the TV was on but Mary seemed to be asleep now, looking so peaceful with her eyes closed, that he didn't want to disturb her. He imagined he would be joining her when he finished his smoke.

Mary was a blind date, set up by his friend Abe, from the office. He had never seen her before tonight. He wondered if he would ever see her again. She didn't really seem like his type any way other than physically and he was pretty sure the feeling was mutual, as evidenced by her current heavy slumber. Joe crushed out his cigarette and, turning out the light, thought, *Christ, I hope she doesn't snore.*

Sleep claimed him in a matter of minutes.

Later, something yanked him from that sleep.

She's just tossing and turning, he thought. He reached over to calm her and, instead, felt something cool and slimy on his fingertips. *Oh, the spot,* he reminded himself. But the spot was moving. Panic gripped Joe and he opened his eyes, groping for the bedside lamp and knocking it off before he could turn it on.

The lamps from the street let in enough pale light for him to see adequately.

Mary lay on her back on the other side of the bed. Her legs were open, her knees forming two mountains beneath the sheet. *Maybe she's ready to go again,* Joe thought. Getting up on his knees, he yanked the sheet back. The panic came back, flushing his cheeks and speeding his heart. The spot had gathered itself up and was halfway inside Mary.

"No," Joe whispered between clenched teeth. A sickening sweat covered his body. Frantically, he reached for the spot, but his fingers went right through it, coming away damp but unable to stop its journey. Feeling like a gynecologist, he got down on his stomach between Mary's legs, watching as the last of the spot slithered up into her.

He collapsed back onto his side of the bed, insane thoughts racing around in his head. By the time he could form a logical thought he had himself convinced it was all a dream. That was impossible, wasn't it? Come couldn't do that, could it? It was shot out of the body and, if it didn't find an egg to fertilize, it died, right?

Joe became aware of Mary's back against his side. See there, it had to be a dream. She wasn't lying like that a few minutes ago. But the thoughts continued to swim around in his head. Reaching over Mary, he rubbed his hand around on the sheet, seeing if he could feel the spot. Feeling nothing, he got out of bed and turned on the light.

Slowly, he walked around to the other side of the bed. *I'll see if that damn thing's still there.* He pulled back the sheet. Bending down close to the mattress, he looked for any sign of it. It was possible that it had dried, he supposed. Midway down the bed he saw something that looked like it could be an outline. The more he looked at it, the more he had himself convinced this had to be the dried stain of the spot. It *was* warm in the room and he *did* have the ceiling fan on its highest setting. It was entirely possible the spot had dried in the hours since it had been expelled from his body. *It was only,* he reasoned, *like a teaspoon of fluid anyway.*

He went back over to his side of the bed, nearly giddy with relief, and turned off the light.

"Is something the matter?" Mary asked.

"No … go back to sleep. I just, I don't know, must have had a dream or something."

"You'll have to tell me about it tomorrow."

"Yeah," he said. "I hope we can laugh about it."

He smoked another cigarette in the dark before closing his eyes and begging sleep to reclaim him.

He woke up later than usual the next morning, feeling well rested. Rolling over, he threw his arm across the empty bed. In Mary's place was a note.

Thanks for everything.

We'll have to do it again sometime.

And her name was signed at the bottom. Joe felt relieved. Even though his dream of last night was little more than a distant memory, he didn't care if he ever saw Mary again.

2.

When he ran into Abe's wife, Shirley, nearly a year later, Joe didn't think he would have even been able to recognize Mary if he saw her. Abe had transferred out of the office and, with that, went any connection to Mary whatsoever. Walking out of a deli with a loaf of bread cradled in his arm, on his way home from the office, he felt a tug at his elbow. He stopped and turned, half-expecting to see a bum wanting a little change.

"Joe Hauser!" Shirley's beaming face met him.

"Shirley," he said. "I haven't seen Abe in forever. How are you guys?"

They stood there in the light drizzle, exchanging small talk about their lives. It amazed Joe how little could happen in a year. Just when Joe was ready to bring the conversation to an end and head home to start his dinner, Shirley turned serious and asked, "Did you hear about Mary Tanner?"

"No. I haven't seen her since that date Abe hooked us up on. How is she?"

"I guess you *haven't* heard. Mary's dead."

"Oh my God. How did that happen?"

"I just heard about it this morning. I don't know if anybody *really* knows what happened. They think she was murdered. Her neighbors in the apartment called the police about sounds of a struggle. The police searched her apartment and, well, there was blood everywhere, but Mary wasn't there."

"Jeez, that's a shame." Joe hated that kind of thing. It had the ability to throw a pall over his entire day. He was beginning to resent Shirley for even bringing it up.

"I'll say it's a shame. I tell you, if they ever catch whoever did that I think he should be tried for double homicide."

"Why's that?"

"Oh, I guess you really hadn't heard about Mary in a while, had you? She was pregnant."

Memories of that night came thudding back to Joe, a flash here, a flash there. *The spot.* He suddenly felt sick.

"That certainly is a tragedy." Joe tried to keep his voice steady. "Listen, if you hear anything more about it, I'd like to know."

"I imagine it'll be all over the papers soon enough."

"I guess so." Joe leaned in and hugged Shirley. "Give my best to Abe. It was nice seeing you."

Shirley returned to her former beaming self. "You need to stop being a stranger, Joe. Come up to the house sometime."

"I'd like that," Joe said, turning to walk home to his apartment.

3.

Joe went home and found himself anxious. He funneled his attentions into an elaborate dinner. It wasn't until it was almost finished that he realized he didn't want to eat alone. He went to the phone and called Melissa who said she would be right over. Joe had not planned on calling Melissa. They had gone out for a few months and she still refused to do more than kiss him goodnight. After leaving her apartment on their last date, Joe found a hooker and sought relief from her. He decided the relationship between him and Melissa was not necessarily a healthy one. But tonight he needed company.

It didn't take her long to get there. They ate dinner in virtual silence and slowly sipped some wine afterward.

"Thank you. That was delicious," Melissa said.

Afraid she was preparing to leave, Joe quickly spat out, "You want to watch a movie?"

"I guess I could stick around. What did you have in mind?"

"You pick."

Together, they went into the living room and Melissa browsed through his collection while he paced around the buffed oak floor.

"You seem agitated. Is something the matter?" she asked, tilted sideways to stare at the movies on his bookshelf.

"No. Well, kind of, I guess. Somebody I know, really more of an acquaintance, died last night."

"That's terrible. You want to talk about it?"

"No. Not really. I really need something to take my mind off of it."

"I'll make sure to pick a comedy."

She brought the DVD over and they sat on the couch, Melissa leaning into him. Joe watched the movie a lot more intently than he probably should have, running his hands through Melissa's dark hair, forcing himself to laugh at parts he thought were supposed to be funny. It wasn't long before she was asleep. Maybe the wine went to her head, Joe thought. He dozed off not too long after thinking that, leaning awkwardly against the arm of his couch.

They both woke up to someone beating on the door.

"Uh, someone's knocking on your door," Melissa said groggily.

"Sounds a little more brutal than knocking," Joe said.

"See who it is. I was getting ready to go, anyway."

Joe didn't want to go to the door. He didn't know why. It was probably just the crazy lady with all the cats from the floor below who wanted to yell at him for having his music up too loud last Tuesday. Surely, he didn't have anything to worry about. Maybe his run-in with Shirley had sparked an impromptu visit from Abe.

The pounding continued as Melissa went into the kitchen to get her coat and purse. When she came back into the living room, Joe was still standing there, staring at the door as it visibly vibrated.

"Come on, open it," Melissa said. "I need to go."

And then the door exploded inward, breaking in half, showering Melissa and Joe in splinters.

"Oh my God!" Melissa screamed.

Joe couldn't even muster a scream. He had expected something, true. He couldn't say what but whatever it was was completely overshadowed by the thing standing in the doorway.

It was the spot, grown to hideous proportions, glistening a whitish-gray. But it wasn't just the spot. Around its waist, as though it had torn straight out of the womb, was Mary. Her middle swelled around the monstrous fetus-like thing's waist, her torso and head hanging down, back to the floor, her eyes milked over, her deathmouth a twisted rictus.

"What is it, Joe?" Melissa asked, grabbing his arms, expecting him to defend her.

The thing continued to move in toward them. Joe grabbed Melissa and pushed her toward the kitchen, not really feeling like they would be much safer in there but at least there were sharp implements, something to defend themselves with. Once in the kitchen, Melissa scrambled toward the phone. Before she could even press the first number, the thing screamed into the kitchen and launched itself at her. Melissa let go a blood-curdling scream that quickly came to a stop. With shaking hands, Joe finished selecting a knife and turned to see the phone sticking out of Melissa's eye socket, a pinkish-gray glop hanging from the antenna that protruded out the back of her skull.

He sprinted out of the kitchen, trying to make it into the hallway. The spot was too fast for him. It pounced on him at the doorway, crushing him under its weight, the back of Mary's head bashing the front of Joe's face hard enough to draw blood. He tried to stab at the thing, but his arms were pinned. Crazily, he thought of that Monty Python movie where John Cleese sings about every sperm being sacred while his army of children dance and sing around him. He wanted to say something to it. Something that might stop it from ending his life but he couldn't think of anything.

What Joe felt next wasn't death. He felt something snaking up his penis and moving around in his lower stomach. He felt a sickening movement down there, like things were being rearranged. All the while, around the head of Mary, Joe watched as the faceless thing stared at him with dim concentration or what Joe thought passed as concentration on that slick, gelatinous caul. Joe felt the thing withdraw from inside him. The spot picked him up and threw him across his apartment, where he crashed into his bookcase and slid into unconsciousness.

4.

Months later, Joe sat on the edge of a bathtub with a razor in his hand. He knew that, in order to do it right, you had to draw it vertically along the veins, really lay them open. His suicide thoughts were based on crazy logic, but nothing else had made sense since that night. There were the police asking about Melissa. There was this hospital where they lobotomized people with drugs. And then there were other things – the morning sickness, the cramping. This morning, Joe was pretty sure he'd felt something move somewhere just below his stomach and when he looked down, he could see the small rounded dome his belly had become. He thought about removing it and realized he couldn't knowingly unleash something like that upon the world. He imagined it slithering up out of the trashcan, ready to destroy anything in its path. He had raided the nurse's station this morning and taken what he felt was an ample amount of pills. Now, with the drugs already dulling his senses he watched as if from someplace else as he drew the blade along his arm from wrist to crook, watching the wound blossom like a long pair of bloody lips.

As he lost consciousness, he felt the thing within him struggle. And, he would never really be sure, but he thought he felt it tearing at the inside of his skin… maybe even breaking free.

Laundrymen

"Have you seen my shirt?" Barry asked.

"Which one?" Michelle returned.

"The brown one. You know, my favorite shirt. The button-down one?"

"Good Lord. It probably curled up and died." She walked over to the blinds in the western-facing window of the apartment, closing them against the last fragments of that day's sun. "Are you sure you washed it? I mean, that thing like never leaves your back. Speaking of which, I think I left my black bra over here the last time. Have you seen *that?*"

"Yeah. Here you go." Barry tossed her the black bra.

The rest of the laundry was organized and sorted on the kitchen table in front of him. He rubbed his forehead.

"No," he said. "I know I washed it. I specifically remember grabbing it from that chair in the bedroom. I'm missing those pants too."

"Which pants?" Michelle collapsed onto the couch, grabbing the remote and turning on the TV.

"The gray corduroys. Have you done something to them?"

"You figured it out, Barry. Yes. I have your clothes. I love them so much that I stole them and, on days that I'm not over here, I'm wearing them all over the place. A big brown shirt and gray corduroys. I'm trying to start a new trend. I hear the frumpy look is coming back in style."

"You don't have to be *so* sarcastic."

"I wasn't being sarcastic. I was being completely serious," she said absently, flipping through the channels. "You probably just left them at the laundromat. Why don't you call?"

"No. I guess I'll just go back over there. That's almost where they have to be. I know I took them. I know I washed them. Probably just left them in the dryer."

Barry grabbed up his keys and headed for the front door.

"You coming?" he asked Michelle.

"Think I'll pass on this one. The Great Clothes Hunt. Nah. Not today. Maybe if it were those jeans I like so much ..."

Barry ran back over to the couch and gave Michelle a quick peck on the mouth. "Be right back."

"I hope your clothes aren't some part of an international conspiracy."

"Never underestimate the power of Mr. Brown."

Michelle chuckled. "Oh my God, you've *named* it."

"I'm very close to it. I'm sure he's been very lonely, trapped in that dryer all by himself."

"But your pants are there to keep him company."

"Still, they shouldn't be left unsupervised."

"You better hurry."

"To the Batmobile."

Then Barry rushed out the door, regretting the fact he had to leave Michelle alone in his little apartment and hoping she would be there when he returned.

Barry rolled the car windows down and enjoyed the early summer breeze as he drove to the laundromat. Children ran throughout the town, happy to be out of school. There weren't any parking spaces directly in front of the laundromat so Barry circled the block and ended up parking a few doors down.

He got out of the car and took in the smell of the clean night air. He looked up at the sky, deepening into purple, casting a twilight glow all around him. Taking his time, he strolled down the sidewalk to the laundromat.

Once there, he stood outside, staring into the laundromat's harsh fluorescent lighting. He didn't know why he didn't just walk right in. Was he hoping to spot his clothes lying around somewhere? Did he think they would have them hanging in the window like some flyer from someone who had found a stray dog?

Barry reached for the door to go inside when he saw the man.

The man, standing back at the line of dryers embedded in the far wall, was wearing Barry's clothes.

That's ridiculous, Barry thought. It's entirely possible someone else has the exact same clothes. Besides, he figured, he wasn't even really close enough to be sure those *were* his clothes adorning the man.

Barry opened the door and stepped into the humidity of the laundromat. Instead of walking directly toward the man, Barry wandered off to his right, around the islands of washers.

Christ, he thought, I'm sneaking up on this man.

And that's exactly what he was doing. The closer he got to the man, the more Barry realized he *had* to be wearing his clothes.

The man was perfectly normal looking, close-cropped black hair, tan skin. Somewhat thinner and shorter than Barry, the clothes were baggy on him.

Barry moved up next to him, prepared to begin his spiel by saying, "Excuse me …"

Just as Barry opened his mouth, the man turned and saw him. Then, lightning quick, he reached out a hand and shoved it into the middle of Barry's chest, taking him by surprise and knocking him to the floor before running through the laundromat's side door. Barry fought to stand up as quickly as he could and follow the man out the door. Now, everyone in the laundromat looked in his direction.

Barry burst through the door and out into the twilight. He saw the man running off to his right and ran in that direction himself.

Barry had not run in a number of years and the man lost him by cutting into the first alley he came to, disappearing into fresh shadows.

"The clothes!" Barry screamed. "They'll never fit you!" As if that statement would cause the thief to have some sort of understanding, some complete change of heart and come running back.

Then Barry had another idea. If the man was at the laundromat, surely he must have some of his own clothes there. When Barry had first approached him, the man was bent over one of the tables. Maybe he was folding his own clothes. He had to have been wearing *something* when he entered the laundromat.

Barry went back into the laundromat, his head hung low, trying to avoid eye contact with all the people who had seen him get shoved down. He crept over to where he had seen the man. He looked for something on the table, the same table Barry had used an hour ago, but didn't see anything. He looked at the row of dryers and saw one with a few meager items lying lifeless at the bottom of the stopped dryer.

Those must be them, Barry thought.

He stepped toward the dryer but just as he got ready to reach out and open the door, a burly woman beat him to it, shooting a dirty glare at him. Barry watched her pull out a giant thong with hearts on it and a blue halter-top. A shiver ran over Barry's skin.

"You can use it now," she barked at Barry. "If that's what you was wantin."

"Thank you," Barry said, but he felt numb. Absently, he turned and wandered out of the Laundromat, back to his car.

By the time he sped back to his apartment and raced up the stairs, Barry was sweaty and out of breath.

"Good God, what's the matter with you?" Michelle asked.

Barry slammed the door behind him, went over to the couch and collapsed onto it. "You're not gonna believe it," he said.

"You should try me."

Michelle was standing, her coat on and her purse slung over her shoulder.

"You look like you're going someplace," Barry said.

"Yeah, Brandon called. He's over at Derek's. Wants me to pick him up. He's been pretty clingy lately. I don't think he wants me and you getting too close, you know. I'll be back tomorrow though. He has school."

"Okay, I'll make it quick."

Barry told her about what had happened at the laundromat, his voice as full of bewilderment as it was of anger.

"Oh well," Michelle said. "Stranger things have happened, I guess. It could have been your wallet or something."

"I know," Barry said, resigned. "It's just, I don't know, it was so fucking odd. I mean, why would he want my *clothes*? Wasn't he wearing any clothes when he came in? Wouldn't somebody have noticed? Who goes to the laundromat to steal people's clothes? Why not dig through dumpsters or something. Did he put them on *over* his regular clothes?"

"Everything doesn't have a rational explanation. You're old enough to know that by now."

"Oh, I'm well aware of that but it's just … *frustrating.*"

"Well, as much as I'd rather stick around and hear you mope about your lost clothes, I'd better go. See you tomorrow." She came over to the couch and kissed him deeply. He ran a hand up the inside of her smooth thigh, beneath her loose skirt.

"Sure you can't stay for a few more minutes?"

"I really have to go. Sorry."

"That's okay." Barry watched her walk out the door, enjoying the view and saddened by her encroaching absence.

With Michelle gone, Barry didn't really have anything to do. He sat on the couch with the television on, unwatched. He couldn't stop thinking about what had happened in the laundromat. The more he thought about it, the more it unnerved him.

He thought about making himself something to eat and then decided he wasn't hungry.

He couldn't even really figure out why it bothered him so much. It wasn't like the clothes were expensive or anything. It wasn't even that they were *his* clothes, or were at one time. He had donated countless items of clothing to the Salvation Army and Goodwill. Hell, there was probably a whole town somewhere adorned in clothes that had once been his.

What bothered him about this incident was that it was almost like this man had gone to great lengths to … *abduct* these clothes. Barry felt like he had been singled out. That's what really bothered him about it – the fact that he was alone in this situation. Never had he heard of anyone else suffering this same problem.

Suffering?

Okay, maybe that was a bit too much. Sure he was a victim, but of what?

Feeling helpless, he switched off the TV, stripped down, and crawled into bed, longing for the nights that Michelle would be there beside him, his nose pressed against her strawberry scented hair…

Barry awoke to a brightly lighted apartment. A quick look around told him it was his, however scarcely recognizable. The couch and coffee table were kicked over. The TV was turned up to full volume, buzzing test patterns of a station that had gone off-air. All of his drawers were opened, clothes strewn everywhere. His closet was gutted. All the cabinets in the kitchen were open, the water faucet in the kitchen sink running full blast.

Three men stood in the middle of the room, staring at him.

One of them was the man he had seen at the laundromat, still wearing Barry's brown shirt and gray corduroys. The other two were also wearing Barry's clothes.

Barry fought the temptation to pull the sheet up around his shoulders and cower back into the bed. Instead, he slung the sheet off, walking up to the three men in all of his nakedness.

He drew very close to the man in the middle, the one from the laundromat and, sounding as authoritative as he could, said, "What the fuck are you doing here?"

"What are *you* doing here?" the man shot back.

"I *live* here."

"It's a shame. The place is a shambles."

"Take off my clothes," Barry demanded.

"These are not your clothes."

"Yes, they are. You stole them from the laundromat. And you two, you must have taken those right out of my closet."

"Actually, they were laying on the kitchen table. And they're not your clothes."

"What do you mean they're not my clothes?"

"We think they fit us better. These should be our clothes. Therefore, they are our clothes."

"You need to leave. Right now."

"No."

"Okay. You know what, fuck it, I'm calling the police. Stealing my clothes is one thing but breaking into my house is another. So I'm calling the police and then I'm going to get out my baseball bat and beat you fuckers until they get here."

"Oh, I wouldn't do that."

Barry went into the kitchen where the phone was. The phone was off the hook and he had to place it on the hook before picking it up again.

Before dialing the "9," Barry asked, "Why wouldn't you do this?"

"Because you're in a lot more trouble than we are."

"I think you're fucking nuts. And I think you're breaking and entering. And I think you've vandalized my entire apartment. I think you're in plenty of trouble."

"But you invited us."

"Like hell I did."

"I don't think you're aware of all the things you've done."

"I don't know what the hell you're talking about. How did you find this place anyway?"

"When a man is running, when he is desperate, he leaves behind a scent, an essence. That's what led me to the laundromat. That's how I found your clothes. And of course, your scent was all over your clothes, embedded in the fabric, smudged against the collar."

"I'm not running from anything."

"Where were you at 3:28 this morning?"

"I was…" Barry looked at the clock on the stove. It read: 3:28. "I was standing in my apartment calling the police on three intruders."

"But we were never here."

And then the apartment was plunged into darkness and quiet.

Barry was back in his bed.

The apartment was more than dark. Barry had the sensation of being somewhere very deep under the sea.

He heard a popping sound. And then another popping sound

and felt himself rising through the sea, toward his apartment, toward his bed that felt like it was at the surface of the water.

Suddenly, he broke through the surface of the sea. Into his apartment. Into his bed.

Barry stood in the middle of the bed, aware that he was holding something heavy. When he looked down, he saw that it was an ax. And what he saw beneath that, pressed down wetly into the bed, caused him to scream.

Michelle was down there only it wasn't the whole Michelle. It was pieces of Michelle, her blood spattered all over Barry's gray pants, wetting the arms of his brown shirt and sticking the fabric to his skin.

She was red and the bed was red and Barry couldn't stop screaming.

The Warm House

School let out early because of the snow. Amy Bradshaw pulled her car to the curb in front of her house. There was already at least a foot of snow on the ground and her cheap car with its bald tires (a perfectly good car for a sixteen-year-old girl, according to her father) had barely made it from the high school. On the way home, she had listened to the weather reports on no fewer than three different radio stations and they all predicted the same thing — blizzard. When it got dark in a few hours, the temperature was expected to drop even further and the winds were supposed to pick up. They were advising businesses to close and motorists to stay off the road. There would be white-outs, the weather people said. They advised against the elderly and the infant leaving their homes.

Great, Amy thought, I'm going to have to be a shut-in for the next three days. Maybe she could go over to a friend's or get one of her friends to come over to her house so she wouldn't have to bear the company of her parents without some kind of a buffer. She was an only child and often hated this fact of life. The fact that she was the only one for her retired parents to focus their considerable attentions on.

My little princess, her dad often called her.

Yes, it seemed like he called her that every chance he got and she was getting sick of it. She no longer wanted to be anyone's princess. Sadly, her parents' affections were making her hate them. Maybe she was just getting older. She wanted to go off to college, someplace very far away and maybe only come back to visit during holidays and summers. She felt bad for feeling these things but, nevertheless, the feelings were there. They brewed to a thick froth with each passing day.

She thought all of this as she sat there in her shit car in front of her (her *parents'*) large house and took a deep breath before getting out. She pulled her coat tight around her neck and decided not to bother grabbing her backpack from the passenger seat. She probably wouldn't need it until Sunday. Today was only Thursday. She counted on school being cancelled tomorrow.

The car door opened with an ancient squeak, wind biting into her skin.

Getting out of the car, she plunged ankle-deep in the snow and cursed it. She went around the front of the car and cautiously walked up the walk leading to her house.

Reaching her front door, she was surprised to find a package waiting below the mailbox. Hopefully, it was something for her. Maybe something she had ordered from the Internet and completely forgotten about.

It was a simple rectangular box sitting with its length vertical. The side of it, in green lettering, read: "OPEN IMMEDIATELY ORGANIC MATTER ENCLOSED."

Maybe someone sent me flowers, she thought. It *was* getting close to Valentine's Day. She quickly laughed that thought away. High school boys were not considerate enough to send packages.

A disappointing affirmation flooded her as she cleared some of the dirt from the address label. These weren't for anyone in her house. The label read "1311 Oakmount Dr." They were for the neighbor. The toad who lived next door. She could probably tell her dad they received a package in error and let him be the one to take it over but Amy thought it might buy her a few more minutes. Not to mention that she would, hopefully, be able to get a glimpse of the way the toad lived. She loved finding out things about people. The man had lived next door for nearly a year and she didn't know anything at all about him. She knew he was ugly, middle-ageish, lived alone, and rarely left the house. This chronic indoorsiness led her to believe he did not have a job. Of course, the neighborhood was relatively affluent so maybe he did something over the Internet. Or maybe he collected disability. Or maybe he lived off an inheritance.

Suddenly, her interest was piqued.

Besides, it was very cold outside and if the box did contain flowers then she didn't think it was such a good idea to leave them sitting out there any longer than was absolutely necessary.

She picked the box up, holding it delicately with both hands, and walked back down the snow-covered walkway. The snow had picked up; big fat flakes that accumulated fast and stuck to the road. Maybe she would walk to Jennifer's later. She was the only one of her friends who lived in the neighborhood and she certainly didn't think she would be driving anyplace for the rest of the day.

Reaching the end of her walk, she turned right and walked the short distance to the neighbor's house on the obscured sidewalk.

Then she turned another right and started up the neighbor's walkway.

Curious, she thought. His house wasn't covered in snow like all the other houses in the neighborhood. The roof gleamed black as though it *had* snowed on it and now the snow had simply... melted off. That didn't seem quite right, she thought, but she guessed stranger things had happened. Maybe it was just the way his house sat or something. Maybe the wind had peeled off most of the snow and she was just imagining it looked wet. It was possible the meager sunlight hit his house in a more direct way than it hit the other houses.

As she reached the porch, she noticed the windows were also steamed up and while this didn't seem exactly normal, it didn't seem to be any reason for her to run screaming or anything. Maybe the guy just liked it warm. And speaking of the guy, she realized she didn't even know his name. Live next door to someone for nearly a year and you don't even know their first or last name. That didn't seem right, either. Suddenly, that seemed just as strange as the lack of snow on the man's roof.

But she had just seen his name, hadn't she? On the mailing label of the box. Why hadn't it stuck with her? She glanced back down at the box.

Brent Johnson, the man's name was. Totally inoffensive and unremarkable. No wonder it had simply bounced off her memory. Sometimes it amazed her how shallow she could be. How could she be truly interested in people and not remember a name, however forgettable, for two minutes?

Oh well. She was cold. She now wanted to be done with this business. Dump the package on the poor old ugly guy, pop in and say "hi" to Mom and Dad and then head on over to Jennifer's. Maybe Jen had managed to score some more vodka from her friend who worked at the drive-thru and they could warm up their evening that way.

Sounded good to her.

She rang the doorbell and waited.

She tapped her foot in the slush at the bottom of the door and rang the bell again.

Waited.

Jesus, it was cold. And the wind had already picked up.

She was about ready to simply set the package on the porch swing to the right of the door when she heard a voice call from inside.

"Coming," it said.

The door swung open and a tired-looking man opened the door. Her breath caught up in her throat. No, she realized, she didn't know anything about this Brent Johnson at all.

What startled her was that he wasn't as ugly as she had imagined. Only he was. She didn't know exactly. It was like he was probably really attractive at one time but, somewhere along the line, scars had happened. A lot of them. His face was covered in a series of thin, spiderweb-like scars, reaching down his neck and into the collar of his shirt. It made her think of looking into a fractured mirror.

Definitely disability, she thought.

He also wasn't as old as she had thought. Certainly not old enough to be retired. He was maybe only ten years or so older than she was. He had beautiful eyes. They were something like blue but not. Or not like any blue she had ever seen before.

She coughed, trying to break her trance. It wasn't her intention to make him feel like some kind of circus freak.

"Umm, sorry, Mr. Johnson. I think this is for you."

Confusion filled his eyes until she proffered the package toward him.

"I think it's flowers or something," she offered. "I didn't think they should be left outside."

Then his eyes lit up and maybe, just *maybe*, there was a little bit of madness there.

"Ah, yes! That's very good indeed. I can't believe they sent them to the wrong house. Come in out of the cold. Please."

"Well, I just live right next door. I'll be okay."

"No, come on in. You have to see this flower. A girl like you should appreciate beauty like this." Her cheeks blushed past their already cold-reddened state. He wiped a hand across his mouth, his eyes now greedily glued to the package. "It only takes a minute to look, right? Besides, we won't see flowers for months around here."

He took the box out of her hands quickly and turned around, heading into the house.

She hesitated for only a second before following him. There was something inviting about his house once she stepped all the way inside. It was incredibly warm, for one thing. Balmy. And it smelled good. She struggled for a second to think of what the smell reminded her of and then she had it. The ocean. Brent Johnson's house smelled like the ocean.

He sat the box down in the center of the oak kitchen table and grabbed a knife from one of the drawers to the right of the sink.

"You're not going to believe this," he said. "I bet you've never seen anything like this at all."

Expertly, he sliced open the box. Rather than just cutting the tape and lifting the flower out of the box, he cut along three edges of the side that faced him. Then he slid the knife out of the box and held it up to the fluorescent light hanging over the table.

"Would you look at that," he said, his eyes sparkling with wonder, his lips turned up in a smile, deepening all of the scars covering his face.

She didn't know what to think. She didn't really pay that much attention to flowers but this one was certainly impressive. It reminded her of an orchid, the way the blooms hung at the end of a long stalk. But the blooms were huge, probably the size of her fist. They were a purple color, deep deep purple and it almost looked like they had been dusted with glitter. And they looked wet, as though something was oozing out of them.

"That's very pretty, Mr. Johnson."

"Oh, please, call me Brent. I'm so sorry. So distracted by the flower that I didn't even get your name."

"Oh, I'm Amy Bradshaw, from next door."

"You must be the daughter."

"That's right. What do you call it? The flower."

"Well, see, that's one of the good things about the flowers *I* collect. They don't have names."

"But I thought people who collected flowers were like obsessed with names."

"Some of them are. Some of us aren't. These flowers don't really come from your standard-type places. I don't know how to explain it, exactly. I think the name removes some of the mystery from them. When I look at my flowers, I see them for what they are. It is more complex and runs deeper than any word could ever describe. Would you like to see some more of my flowers?"

"Sure, I guess." She didn't think it would do any harm and she found herself feeling pretty comfortable in this house and, besides, what could possibly happen with her parents right there next door?

She followed him through the house and down into his brightly lighted basement.

What she saw down there hit her all at once. She felt like she was going to be sick but, for some reason, she didn't run.

"When you woke up this morning," Brent said. "Did you ever think you were going to die?"

This knocked her even further off guard.

She tried to back up but could barely move. She felt limp. The heat or bright lights or the things dangling from the walls stole something from her. I feel wilted, she thought, collapsing onto the bottom stair, desperate and terrified. Those weren't the only things she felt. Somewhere deep inside of her sparked the smallest grain of excitement. Or maybe it was adrenaline. She didn't know, didn't have time to analyze it. She only knew that it was something she hadn't felt in a very long time.

"You don't really want to leave," Brent said, wiping his mouth in that way that made her think he needed a drink of water.

Maybe he was right, she thought. At least, for now, maybe it was best to make him *think* he was right. It would give *her* time to think of a way out.

Tasting bile in the back of her throat, she looked around the brightly lighted basement. The gentle cerulean walls were only a background to the horrors standing out from them – a mixture of exotic plant life and human death. Or something like death. She wasn't really sure if the people hanging, pressed against the walls, were dead or not. Dismembered certainly, but maybe not dead. If they *were* dead, then they had been preserved remarkably well. Their skin still shone. Some of them appeared to breathe.

But everything breathes if you stare at it long enough.

She counted to ten.

Whatever they were or whoever they had been, they were something else now... That something else wasn't as disgusting as she had initially found it to be. The closer she looked at them, the more beautiful they became.

Across the basement in front of her hung a woman. Her left arm was gone. A thick, bright green vine grew out of the shoulder, as if replacing the arm. In place of her eyes were two deep blue blooms, undoubtedly larger than her eyes had ever been. A dark green carpet covered her legs. Was it some kind of moss? Amy wondered.

To the woman's left was another figure. She couldn't tell if it was male or female. Its head was thrown back in something like revelation or ecstasy. The body's torso was either missing or hidden, serving as fertilizer in some form of sick flowerbed. In its place, in a sloppy vertical line, grew three bright orange blossoms.

She should have turned and run. She knew this. She wanted to. Everything inside of her, everything in her being except for that wilted feeling and that spark of excitement, told her she *had* to get out of this place.

"Lovely, isn't it?" Brent asked her.

"Are they... are they dead?" Her voice was thick. It was an effort to push out any sound at all.

"Dead? No, they're not dead. They won't be coming back to this world anytime soon, though. They have gone some other place."

"Where did they go?"

"Well, I can't say exactly. I've only seen it in glimpses myself. I think of it as the land of the flowers. That's where all of these come from. The flowers take you to the land and they come from this land and it is all very confusing. The flowers are not very good at, uh, invoking clarity. And this land... it... *changes* with each flower."

He stopped talking and surveyed the basement, as though drinking in the ugly beauty surrounding him.

"Perhaps I'm getting ahead of myself," he said. "See, this place, I can only get there by consuming the flowers. I don't know where the flowers come from. I *think*... I *think* they come from over there. It wasn't until I moved here that I started getting them. Each month, these boxes would show up. The first one had instructions in it. Very explicit instructions on how to eat them. It was like something out of *Alice's Adventures in Wonderland*. I had to try it. The first time, I tried it alone. It changed me. I won't lie to you. I haven't been the same man since. But, after that first time, I knew it wasn't something I wanted to do alone. No, it was something I wanted to share. And that's why the others are down here. I know it looks like I have done something bad to them but, truthfully, I don't know if it is all that bad. And I can tell by the look on your face that *you* think I've done something bad to them. So maybe I have but... well, let me ask you this..."

He crossed the room and held his hand in front of one of the flower figures, one with a radiant and fleshy purple bush for a head.

"Does *this* sound like pain?"

He rubbed his hand down the figure's side. A moan came from somewhere on the figure, perhaps somewhere in the bush that had replaced her mouth. It certainly wasn't a moan of pain. Amy had made moans like that with her first and only boyfriend. But it went even beyond the moans she had given her boyfriend. The moans she had given her boyfriend were more for his benefit and ego. This moan escaping the woman hanging from the wall... *that* moan was what an orgasm would sound like, Amy thought.

"Now I have to ask you if you would like to go to this place with me. I won't lie to you. You might end up just like these people. I really don't know. Maybe it's happiness. Maybe it's misery. I wouldn't know, because I'm never allowed to stay. No matter what happens, I always come back. I don't know why it happens. I don't really even know what happens when I'm over there. I just know that I come back and I have more scars to mark my voyage and a sense of longing greater than any need I have ever had before. But *these* people... these people are there all the time."

Amy didn't know. She didn't feel like she had a whole lot of time to decide. In front of her sprawled a fate that was horrifying yet wild, mysterious, and potentially pleasurable while, out there, well, *out there* just seemed so boring now. How could she ever go back *out there* without having at least given this a chance?

She knew that was what every addict thought when trying their chosen vice for the first time.

A thick sweat had greased her skin since coming to the basement. She felt light-headed. She raised her head up from between her knees and said, "I'll go. Just tell me what you want me to do."

As she spoke the words, she was surprised. That was not what she wanted to say. Clearly, something had happened to her since coming down here and now a sudden panic gripped her. What if this enchantment could not be undone? What then?

Now, even while thinking about how much she wanted to quit this insanity, she spoke again, "What do you want me to do?"

"Oh, well, it's nothing too complex. You are the youngest one to go with me. That concerns me a little bit. See, when I told you before that I didn't name flowers, well, that was a little bit of a lie. The flowers all had names to begin with."

He walked over to one of the figures that had something like calla lilies growing down her left leg and patted her. She moaned as his hand touched her.

"This one," he said. "Is named Monica. That one..." he pointed to the one next to her. "Is named Celina." He pointed to one on the far side of the room. "And that one, unfortunately, is named Tonya."

Then he held out the flower that came for him today, elevating it under the bright fluorescent light so the light caught on the sparkles covering the petals. "And this one," he said. "I suppose this one will be called 'Amy.'"

He plucked off two of the petals, balancing them gingerly on the tips of his index and middle fingers.

"All you have to do is eat this. It doesn't really take any time at all."

Slowly, he crossed the basement toward her. Swiping the back of his right hand across his mouth, he extended his left toward her, the petals softly sitting on the tips. A cough would have sent them spiraling to the floor.

Without hesitation, she reached out her own hand, taking one of the purple petals into her slender fingers. More to fully savor the experience rather than any sort of cautionary measure, she held the petal up to her nose and inhaled a deep breath. It smelled like fruit. No fruit that she could place immediately, but it smelled fresh and wonderful, whatever it was. Brent stuck the remaining petal onto his tongue and chewed it slowly. Following his lead, she did the same, thinking of it as some kind of bizarre communion wafer.

An impossible amount of juices splashed the inside of her mouth. It didn't seem right that something so small as a flower petal could contain that much liquid and that much intense flavor. The potency of the flavor was almost biting but there was an underlying sweetness there. That sweetness, that was something she immediately wanted more of. She had the instant urge to run to the plant sitting on the floor of the basement and begin pulling the petals off and shoving them into her mouth. She forgot about Brent entirely. The only thing she wanted at that moment was to have another taste of that flower because the petal she had put into her mouth was already gone, all dissolved, and it had taken its taste with it, rudely gobbling it up like a miser, leaving nothing in its place. Nothing. And this sense of nothingness felt even greater because what it was the alternative to was so great...

Amy wasn't in the basement anymore.

She didn't know how that happened. The plant had taken her to this other place. Instead of the rich sweetness of its taste, the plant now offered her this dreamscape.

She stood in the street, in front of Brent's house, her own house behind her. Theirs was a dead end street and she should have been staring into a field on the other side of a rusted barb-wire fence but what she stared at instead was a vast ocean. It was a beautiful blue ocean. More beautiful than the waters she had seen in travel brochures for the Caribbean. And above the ocean sprawled a sun-filled deep blue sky. What made this odd was that, where *she* stood, on her street, she stood in ankle-deep snow and darkness. She should have been cold but she wasn't. She was merely filled with the desire to walk toward the ocean, to feel its warm waters wrap around her.

She was aware of something else too. She didn't know where it came from exactly. It felt like something else opened up in the back of her head. It was like a window. She didn't understand it. She didn't know if she *wanted* to understand it.

In this window, this spooky ghostplace at the back of her head, she saw Brent. At first, she was afraid he could see her and then she realized he wasn't paying any attention to her whatsoever and even if he *was* there wasn't really any physically possible way he could be living inside her head. At least, she didn't *think* there was. But her thoughts still didn't seem entirely her own.

He looked at himself in a mirror and smiled, as though he were posing for a picture. When he smiled, all of the scars on his face bunched up, making him nearly repulsive. He was naked to the waist and the same scars etched their way across his pale torso. He held a large knife in his hand. He placed the blade to the right corner of his mouth and pulled the knife toward his ear so the skin opened up into a gaping red wound. Then he did the same to the other side, blood running down his neck and onto his chest. Now he would be smiling whether he liked it or not... permanently.

The result was monstrous.

What was the point of all this? Amy wondered. But she only wondered what the point of Brent's actions were. They seemed so tragic and awful compared to what lay in front of her. What lay in front of her didn't make her feel bad at all. It made her feel ecstatic. She ran along her road, the wind whipping around her body, oblivious to its cold sting. Running like that, *thinking* about the one simple act of left leg-right leg, took her mind's eye away from the glowering image of Brent.

Her road ended in a cliff tumbling straight down into the ocean's depths. What lay just beyond that cliff was what really captured her attention. What she saw was something that looked like an island paradise. Only the island was very small. Perhaps the size of her backyard. And it was as high up as the cliff, tottering there, the top of it fatter than the bottom. Amy didn't think it would take much to knock it over. But she planned to go there.

The window in the back of her head opened up again so she could see what Brent was doing. He was in his basement.

Blood covered him. In one hand he held the same butcher knife he had used to slice his face and in the other hand he held a huge pair of gardening shears.

It took her a second to realize what he was doing.

He was *pruning* the women in the basement. The pruning shears went *snip-snip* with great dexterity, taking a leaf here and a finger there, flesh and vegetation treated as though they were the same. Then he leaned over them, the blood spilling from his wounds, "watering" them.

How long would it take him to realize she wasn't there? How long would it take him to realize he didn't have the latest flower he needed? The latest flower he *desired*?

For a second, she contemplated running back to her parents, charging through the front door and telling them about everything that was going on. But she didn't do that. She didn't think it would help. Didn't even know if it would be possible. Besides, she didn't think she was in any condition to know what was going on herself. She imagined herself jabbering on, half-incoherent, spouting nonsense about thoughts not being her own.

What she wanted was the island beyond the cliff in front of her.

In her mind, she watched as Brent sliced an earlobe from one of the women. The woman cried out in some kind of ecstatic agony and something resembling a poppy took the place of the earlobe.

Above Amy, the sky was dark and purple, clouds ominously swirling. In front of her, the blue sunfilled sky. She wanted that.

She stood at the edge of the cliff and opened up her arms to the sky, opened her arms to the wind, letting it take her, letting it gather itself around her clothes, bearing her up and toward that island.

She closed her eyes, smelling the sea as she crossed overtop of it, hearing the waves crash down on the rocks below.

Then she felt ground beneath her feet, smelling the fragrant jungle around her.

She opened her eyes and gagged.

The view around her was similar to the view in Brent's basement only a thousand times worse.

Amy knew these people were not living. That was impossible. Maybe their bodies experienced some kind of unknown sensual pleasure but none of it was of their own choosing any longer and she didn't think that could be considered life.

She didn't want to be on the island anymore.

But she didn't know if she had a choice or not.

She turned to go back the way she had come but Brent blocked her path.

How did he get there? she wondered.

It wasn't important, she figured.

He moved up close to her, grabbing her around the waist. She smelled his blood. It opened up her nose and poured through her body in a way none of the flowers could.

"Let me go," she said, still choking.

"Where do you want to go?" Brent said, his ghastly smile directly in front of her face.

And suddenly, much like the window in her mind that allowed her to see what Brent was doing, something else opened up and she thought she knew what he was thinking. He wanted her to stay here with him. He wanted her to be his queen in this sick warped world of half-life and half-death. He wanted her to let him slide that giant knife down her skin, open up a vein and let her blood spill out so he could drink it. So he could absorb a little more of the things growing around him.

"I just want to go home," she muttered.

"I think you'll like my home much better."

"No," she muttered. She tasted doom on the back of her throat. He seemed so much stronger than her. She struggled against him but it didn't seem to do any good. He could drag her down into the soft dirt and do whatever he wanted to do with her.

But then his grip lessened somewhat and a hurt look blossomed in his eyes.

Amy took this chance to stumble back from him and his blood-spattered knife.

Behind him stood, if one could call it that, something that was half-man and half-bush. His arms were missing. In their place were two vines with lavender flowers dangling from them. And beneath the lavender flowers were thorns no fewer than six inches long. This man wrapped one of his arms around Brent's neck.

Amy wondered if Brent was the one who had created these awful things or if he was just fulfilling someone else's destiny. She turned away from the scene, away from the island, running toward its edge. She stopped at the lip of the island, teetering over the drop and the ocean below.

The ocean wasn't there, she told herself. The ocean had never been there because all of her thoughts were her own and the person who was thinking all those other thoughts for her was left to deal with his own nightmarish fate now. Holding out her arms, she let herself fly into the blue day, sinking slowly down to the warm waves that were not there.

She woke up on the floor of Brent Johnson's basement. No sign of the plant people were down there, just the strangely cerulean walls that now seemed comforting. Maybe she had just come down here and passed out somehow. Maybe the whole thing had been a dream.

She stood up, the aches and pains in her body telling her it wasn't just a dream. Her throat felt scorched. She felt cold.

She walked up the stairs and through the house. The house was bare, like no one had ever lived there, like there had never been a person named Brent Johnson.

Out of the house, she continued to walk, into the snow, the cold scalding her tender skin. She didn't bother with the sidewalk, she walked straight through the yard and up to her porch.

A box sat beneath the mailbox to the right of the door. She recognized the printed message on it. She cleared off the address label, half-expecting to see next door's address on there. Instead, what she saw was her name and her address.

Strangely, she found herself tempted to open it. She wanted, so desperately, to know what was inside the box. But she already knew what was inside the box. She wanted to taste it. She wanted to feel it run through her. But she didn't want to go where it wanted to take her.

Picking up the box, she marched around to the back of the house and put it into the trashcan with the address label facing down so it was just a box and nothing her parents would be too suspicious of.

Then she took a deep breath of the cold, let it fill her lungs, pulled a forbidden cigarette from the pocket of her coat and lit it, looking around at her mundane little neighborhood, all covered in snow and the first thin strands of dusk.

Bury the Children in the Yard

The Filthiest Thing He Had Ever Read

It was the filthiest thing he had ever read. Being an English professor, he'd read a lot. The students' final essays were a small stack on his desk. He had kept hers on top, reading it over and over. Now he moved it to the bottom of the stack and glanced up at the class. The room was too bright. The winter sky gray beyond the windows. Everyone in the room looked depressed. No one even paid attention to him. They just wanted to go home. All of their heads were bowed, texting, staring at whatever small screen they held in their hands. A few of them were hastily scrawling things or reading through some other text book. Probably preparing for another exam they were taking later in the day.

Except her. Ashley Burroughs. She stared right at him. He glanced back down at the stack of essays, caught his breath, pretended to scrawl something on one of them.

Her essay had come completely out of the blue. Even now, she sat in the middle of the class, wearing a skin tight white sweater, a plaid skirt, knee socks and, dear god, brown saddle shoes and pig tails. And she still managed to look innocent rather than trashy. Until last night, he had thought she was a post-secondary student. But he had looked her up in the student database. Nineteen. He couldn't believe he was thinking about going through with this.

Once he was sure his erection had subsided, he cleared his

throat, took the essays in hand, and stood up.

"You're, um, free to go when you get your essay. And welcome to email me with any questions you might have."

He placed the essays on the students' desks. Most of them merely glanced at the final grade and either sighed with relief or grumbled with disappointment. Most of the grades were good to average. In the back left of the classroom sat Paul Skink. He had pulled a brilliant essay off the Internet and printed it out. Didn't bother typing it. Didn't bother reformatting it.

"Really, Paul... " He put the essay in front of the boy, an 'F' marked in red followed by a half page diatribe. The kid guffawed, stood up, and walked slowly from the room.

Eventually, the only student left was Ashley. He had felt her eyes following him around the room. He wouldn't have thought anything of her essay if he hadn't been mentioned by name. Calling it an essay wasn't even accurate. It was really more like a pornographic story and again, if he, if they *both*, had not been mentioned by name, he would have just thought it was something written to grab attention with its offensive content. It was, however, remarkably free of typos and, at the end, she had written in pink ink: "I've wanted you to fuck me all year." Even if she had been a bad student or a different type of person, he would have just thought she was trying to lure him into something. Normally he wouldn't even contemplate something like this. But it had been a very long time since he'd had any kind of female contact. A long time since he'd seriously even considered it. It had been a long time for a lot of things.

"Ashley." He came up behind her and put the essay down on her desk.

"Yes, Mr. Brown?"

"That was, uh, quite a piece of writing."

She looked at the essay, noticed the 'A' written on it, and said, "Thank you."

"Did you, uh, *mean* what was written in there?"

"Yes, Mr. Brown."

"You mean... you would like to actually *do* that stuff?"

The tiniest of smiles curled her mouth. "Yes, Mr. Brown."

He glanced at the door to make sure no one within earshot was loitering there.

"I have a cabin out by the lake. Would you be interested in spending your winter break with me?" His heart pounded. He couldn't believe he just asked her that. He was a fifty-two year old man. He was this girl's professor. He knew he was completely out of line.

"I would like that very much, Mr. Brown."

"Please call me Steve."

"Okay."

"All right then. How bout we meet at Phuong's around noon tomorrow?"

She nodded. Her smile broadened.

"And wear your hair in pigtails again. I want something to hold onto when I fuck you from behind." His heart raced and he could feel his erection blossoming again. He walked back to the front of the room and began putting his papers and his laptop into his messenger bag. He watched her uncross her legs, catching just the briefest glimpse of white underwear. Her nipples stood against her sweater. She may have been blushing slightly. She swung her backpack over her shoulder, held her essay against her chest, and left the room. Steve exhaled a breath it felt like he'd been holding for the past five minutes.

He Was Content to Muddle Along in His Sad Existence

He got in his battered car and drove home through the gray Ohio evening. The college was not a city college. It was a small college in a small college town. He drove down Main Street, past all the historical homes, their windows glowing warmly. He imagined the happy families inside. Families gathering at home for the holidays over good food, strong drink, and warm fires. Many of the houses, he knew, were owned by professors just like him. Some of the more expensive homes were owned by the administrators and the department heads. He could have been one of them. It would have been so easy to become one of them. But a long time ago, something had derailed. He could pinpoint it but he didn't like to do that. At least not consciously. He was content to muddle along in his sad existence and didn't want to seem like the victim.

He turned off Main Street, into college housing now. Some of the houses were just as large but there was a generally squalid quality to most of them, owned by landlords who didn't really care and rented by people who would be living there for nine months at the most, sometimes two or three or more to a bedroom. Then he was away from the town and into the country, on his way to his shabby apartment in a trashy Dayton suburb.

He wondered when his heart was going to stop racing.

Neither Nabokov Nor Coltrane

It was dawn before he finally fell asleep. He kept thinking that what had happened in his classroom with Ashley couldn't have possibly happened. He was drawn tight with sexual tension and had to fight the urge to masturbate, a desire he gave into daily, sometimes more than once. It was a desire that made him feel invigorated and alive because he knew it wouldn't be around forever.

Nothing ever was.

He'd been reading Nabokov's *Invitation to a Beheading* and, by the time he decided to go to bed, realized he hadn't digested a word. The John Coltrane record he'd been listening to had stopped a while ago. Even the irritating sounds of the white trash neighborhood – arguing, drunken yelling, dogs barking, sirens, shitty cars with bad exhaust systems – had gone unnoticed. He couldn't stop thinking about Ashley. It was always the quiet ones. He knew she wouldn't expect anything more than a few days with him, but she hadn't seemed the type. Normally her hair was not worn in pigtails but down. It was a coppery brownish color and wildly curly. She was what most her age probably referred to as "cute" rather than "hot." Apparently cute was his type. While he made it a habit of covertly ogling students she was someone he found himself returning to. And sometimes he had even fantasized about her during his masturbation sessions. The word "ripe" often popped into his head when he looked at her. She was perfect, right now, at this age. She dressed mostly conservatively. Even what she wore today, if not such a cliché, would have been considered conservative. Hell, it was still the uniform at a lot of Catholic high schools. Sometimes he would play a game where he looked at his students and imagined the rest of their lives for them. He saw Ashley dating around in college. Mostly friends of friends. She wasn't a bar type. Not a hookup type. She would graduate college and maybe begin work on a master's degree, but her first priority would be to find some sort of boring, stable job. If she were lucky, it would even pay for her education. She would eventually meet someone she met at work or through a coworker. Someone who was verifiably economically stable and emotionally sound. By this time, she would be carrying a few extra pounds. Still cute but no longer ripe. The type of woman you *know* is going to get fat. She would eventually marry someone who was basically just like her and it wouldn't really matter anyway. At this point, both of their biological clocks would be ticking so loudly for them to both fall into their particular demographics they would appropriately mold and sacrifice parts of themselves to mesh perfectly. She would have a child and, if post-partum depression didn't fuck with her too much and jeopardize the marriage and if she were allowed to quit her job and stay home, another one. But then it would be time for the husband to get a vasectomy and, at this point, it would be her and her children with the husband as a minor accessory.

Dismal.

By the time he got into bed, his lustful thoughts had turned to guilt and he went to sleep thinking about the accident. Nothing turned dreams into nightmares more than that.

The Specific Reason Both of Them Were There

He awoke at ten, made some strong coffee, and watched CNN for about an hour before heading to the Vietnamese restaurant on the outskirts of campus. He thought that would be a safe spot since most of the other students would either be engaged in their last day of finals or on the way home. Phuong's was usually empty anyway.

Ashley wore a spring green wool peacoat, black snow boots, thick white leggings that stopped above her knees and, as requested, the skirt and pigtails. She waited in front of the restaurant. Steve did his best job of parallel parking, which was still laughable, and got out. He'd been trying to think of something to say and ended up managing only, "Hungry?"

"Starved," Ashley said.

They went inside to eat and make small talk. Comments about the weather. What the other one was going to order. Ashley stripped off her coat. She wore a simple white blouse unbuttoned to reveal just the slightest bit of her cleavage. It was enough for Steve. He tried not to stare at her breasts pressing against the shirt. Padded bras left so much to the imagination.

"So why aren't you going home over break?" He hesitated to ask this, thinking it might be something financial. At their school that wasn't usually much of a problem but there were still plenty of students there on financial aid. Financial aid didn't cover plane tickets.

She shrugged. "Mom and Dad travel. They're in Barbados until March. They offered to fly me out there but, I don't know, it seemed like a hassle."

So money definitely wasn't the problem. "Barbados in December sure beats the hell out of Ohio. Might be worth the hassle."

"Ah, yes, but you're not there."

And she had immediately drawn his attention to the specific reason both of them were there. He almost choked.

"Well, yes, um, I'm certainly glad you decided to stay behind."

"Have you ever fucked a student before?"

Jesus. He could feel himself blushing. Felt relieved when the waitress brought a plate of spring rolls. But he wasn't off the hook.

"So... have you?"

"Not, uh, not since I was one."

She laughed.

"Have you ever, uh, done something like this with a teacher?"

She picked up a spring roll, licked her lips, and said, "It's never been something I've wanted before."

He picked up a spring roll and took a bite, noting she didn't directly answer his question.

They both finished eating fairly quickly. He put her coat on for her, took a deep breath of her hair. He opened the car door for her, waited for her skirt to slide up as she sat in the seat. Then they were on their way to his modest cabin on Furnace Lake, the maintenance of which was the one indulgence he had ever allowed himself. It was one he thought he had paid for every day of his life but he couldn't seem to part with it. On the ride there, he kept wondering why he didn't just take her back to his apartment, bang the hell out of her, and be done with the whole sordid affair.

Maybe she deserved more than that but, in the end, he thought the result would be about the same.

The cabin was about an hour away in the opposite direction of the college. Otherwise, he wouldn't have bothered wasting the money to rent his shitty apartment and lived in the cabin year round. The radio was on NPR and he considered asking her what she planned on doing when she graduated just to make polite small talk. He stopped himself, cleared his throat, and said, "So I probably don't need to really bother with much conversation, huh?" He thought of that story she had written. Whoever she was on the outside was not reflected in that story. Maybe she had tried to show him what she really thought. How she wanted life to be. Who was he to argue with that?

"Not really. Unless you want to."

"Maybe later. But not so much right now. I *cannot* stop thinking about fucking you." He glanced over at her. Long enough to catch the smirk and the hint of color flushing her cheeks.

"I've been wet since meeting you at the restaurant."

He grabbed her hand and put it on his thigh. More female contact than he'd had in over a decade.

She scooted toward him in her seat and moved her hand up his thigh until she found his penis. It was hard and she began rubbing it lightly. It stiffened further. He looked down at her hand. Dull silver rings on her thumb and index finger.

Her thigh was warm on his free hand. He moved it up to her crotch. Even warmer. Her underwear were damp. He wanted to go inside them, but he also enjoyed torturing himself. He found the outline of her labia and began tracing it with his pinky.

"Are you thinking about my pussy?" Her whisper was full of

warm moist breath that reached into his skull.

"Yes."

"You feel pretty hard. Are you thinking about being inside me... Steve?"

He continued to lightly rub her. "Actually, I'm just thinking of your pussy. What it looks like. What it tastes like."

"And you're so busy driving right now."

"A shame."

She unfastened her seatbelt, unbuttoned and unzipped his pants. He lifted his ass up off the seat and she tugged his jeans and underwear down past his scrotum, his penis springing free. She dipped her finger in the pre-come gathered at the tip and smeared it around.

"You have a fine looking cock."

"Thanks."

"Have you ever done something like this?"

"I was young once, too... and married. I've done just about everything. But that was a *very* long time ago."

"Whatever girls you've had, I'm not like them."

"No?"

"No."

"Show me."

"What are you going to do if I don't?"

He wanted to tell her that was okay. It would be all right if she just wanted to talk. But he thought she must be playing with him. Her story had them doing some pretty sick stuff.

He didn't say anything.

She rested her chin on his shoulder. "What if I didn't exist? I mean, like what if I didn't have any feelings? And what if no one was watching and you never had to answer for your actions? What if the only thing you had to worry about was your next orgasm? What if that was the only thing that existed?" She wrapped her hand around the length of his cock. "Boys my own age are kids. I get bored with them. I'm only doing this because I thought you might have enough experience and imagination to make it interesting. I'm a sick sick girl."

He took his hand from between her legs and grabbed one of her pigtails.

"Put it in your mouth."

She maneuvered around in her seat until sitting on her knees. She leaned over him. He focused on the road, feeling her tongue run up the length of his cock. She stuck the tip of her tongue against the opening of his penis. She opened her mouth and took the head of his penis in. He grabbed the back of her head, pushed it down until she gagged, then let go. He thought of his dick in her mouth, in her throat. She continued to bob her head up and down, slowly. He was almost shaking. He didn't think he could reach an orgasm while he was driving and still stay on the road. The next pull off he came to, he turned the car into it and put it into park. He let his seat back and used both of his hands to press her head down on his cock. He leaned back and began pumping his hips toward her face. She gagged but made no attempt to back off. He went faster and harder, feeling his penis in her spasming throat. Then he thrust and held it while he came. She backed off, coughed, retched, and wiped some come from her bottom lip. Her eyes were watery but she smiled at him.

"See. Not so hard." Her voice was raspy.

He grabbed her head and pulled her toward him, kissing her, tasting maybe a bit of himself on her tongue.

They both readjusted themselves and he pulled back onto the road. She asked him if it was okay if she smoked. He said sure. It really didn't bother him. If it had, he would have told her no. He almost told her no anyway.

There was a small carry-out a few miles from the cabin. He stopped there, told her to wait in the car, and went in for some fruit, wine, beer, lunch meat, and bread. It had been a while since he'd had to worry about feeding anyone. He also paid for a couple bundles of wood for the cabin's fireplace. Maybe it would be a good touch.

He Didn't Want to Tell Himself It Was Guilt

It was still light when they reached the cabin. Steve didn't think either of them had spoken since he'd come out of the carry-out. Ashley sat there beside him, and he was very aware of that, but he still felt a million miles away. There was something else inside of him too. He didn't want to tell himself it was guilt. Not after all these years. That would have been ridiculous. The cabin was one of many others surrounding the huge Furnace Lake. The spot was still heavily wooded and mostly invisible from the other cabins. Not that it mattered this time of year. It helped give him the illusion that Furnace Lake wasn't one of the biggest vacation destinations of the area in the summer. Not that that really meant much in Ohio. There were maybe a couple of boat and bike rental places, the carry-out, a tiny movie theater in what consisted of Furnace Lake's downtown. The theater, like most of the businesses in town, was only open Memorial Day through Labor Day.

He unlocked the door and opened it for Ashley. He flipped a light switch and turned the thermostat on the electric baseboard heat up. Soon the place would smell like burning dust, not a completely unpleasant smell. They put their bags on the kitchen counter and he plugged the refrigerator in and pushed it back against the wall.

"Nice," Ashley said. "Cozy."

"Thanks. It's not much. Been in the family for years."

He rinsed out a couple of coffee mugs, uncorked the wine, and poured a little in each glass. He handed her one of them. She took it with her free hand. The other hand held her phone. A slight smirk tilted her face.

"This probably isn't the best stuff in the world," Steve said. She dismissively nodded at him. "Uh, miss a lot of calls?"

She put the phone in a pocket in her skirt. "No one under thirty calls anyone anymore."

"Ah, yes, texting. An art that never found me."

"I've always found it interesting how reluctant bookish types are to take up texting. It seems like it was made for you."

"Maybe it's because of what it does to the English language. Or maybe it's because we're so quiet most of the time it's occasionally more exciting to open our mouths. Probably good you have that though. In case of emergencies. I don't have a cell phone or a landline here. Keeps it peaceful."

She took a gulp of the wine. "I'm still kind of wet." She set the glass back on the counter.

He polished his wine off and put his hands around her upper arms, leading her to the one bedroom in the back of the house. This room was the smallest and was already pleasantly warm. He turned her to face him and leaned her toward the bed until she lay on her back. This was going to be like unwrapping a present. He wanted to do it a little at a time.

He parted her knees and lifted up her skirt. She wore boy brief underwear, black and trimmed in white. He slowly pulled them down. She had absolutely no pubic hair. He didn't mind this at all, although it was the first time he'd actually seen it in the flesh. He kneeled between her legs.

"So what do you think?" she asked. "It looks like a peach that's been sliced open, doesn't it?"

He looked at it and considered. Then he nodded. "But let's hope it tastes like you."

He kissed all around it, gently sucking and biting in certain places, before running his tongue along the labia, teasing the clitoris, and eventually plunging his tongue inside of her. Her moans seemed to come from very far away. She writhed her hips and he cupped her ass with his hands. He alternately tongued her and sucked away the excess come. Her hands were gripping the back of his head.

He pulled back and said, "I want to watch you play with yourself now."

He pulled her skirt the rest of the way off and moved one of her hands between her legs. She slowly began massaging herself with her fingertips. He stripped off his clothes and went to the head of the bed. He slowly unbuttoned her shirt and unfastened her bra. Her breasts were full and perfectly formed, the nipples an innocent shade of pink. He took one of them in his mouth, massaged the other one with one of his hands, and stroked himself with his remaining hand. She moaned and said his name. Eventually they got under the covers and he slid into her for the first time. They went slow. He was gentle at first. As he approached orgasm, he grabbed her behind the knees, forcing her legs to either side of her head while he pounded into her and she continued moaning that gradually escalated into screaming.

They lay in bed and held each other for a while before getting up to get something to eat. She checked her phone again and typed off a message in return. Before going back into the bedroom, he made her leave it in the kitchen.

"I notice you didn't bring any kind of bag," he asked.

"Well, I didn't think I'd really need the clothes and I wasn't sure how long we'd be here. I figure you have a shower."

"That I do."

"I'm a light packer. I don't like to be responsible for a lot of stuff."

When they went back into the bedroom, he spanked her until her skin was hot and red, and then he fucked her in the ass. Afterward, she went to the bathroom and he dozed off. Had the dream.

Obsession and Insanity

He woke up momentarily disoriented. Once he realized he was in the cabin and remembered *why* he was in the cabin, everything seemed to become even more of a dreamlike blur. His eyes were open but it was so dark they may as well have still been closed. He reached over to feel the other side of the bed. Ashley wasn't there.

He hadn't bothered setting the clock in the room, never wore a watch, and didn't have a cell phone so he had no idea what time it was. He was still completely naked. He swung his legs over the edge of the bed, felt around for his pants, and slid them on. He pulled on his sweater and socks, remembering it would be pretty chilly outside the room.

He went out to the main part of the cabin, expecting to find a light on, Ashley maybe sitting on the couch and reading or something. It was dark and he didn't see any sign of her.

The porch light shone in through the front door. He didn't remember turning it on so he opened the door and leaned out. Ashley sat in one of the wooden deck chairs, texting something and smoking.

"There you are," he said.

She looked at him. It looked like she'd been crying. "Yep."

He looked out over the dark lake. It had warmed considerably, not at all unusual for Ohio, and a fog was rolling in. There probably wouldn't be any visibility come dawn.

"You going to be out here a while?"

She held up her cigarette for an answer.

"Let me grab some shoes. Need anything?"

"I'm okay."

He slipped his shoes on, went to the kitchen to grab the bottle of wine, noting that it had been depleted considerably since their earlier glasses, and grabbed a fleece blanket off the back of the couch.

He set the blanket on Ashley's lap and said, "Thought you might be cold."

"Thanks."

He uncorked the bottle with his teeth and sat down in the chair beside hers. A chill went up his spine. This was too familiar. He wanted to tell her to go grab her things, they needed to go, and then he remembered she hadn't brought anything. He thought maybe that made it even weirder. Like she could just move right in and take Heidi's place. Like that was what he'd been waiting for for the past twenty years. The dream still rode his brain hard. He took a healthy slug of the wine. It would either help the dream fade or set the bear trap his mind had become, waiting to obsessively snap down on the littlest thought and stay clamped until it twitched its last.

But it would never twitch its last. Steve knew that.

"Couldn't sleep?" Steve asked.

"Didn't try."

"You're being very laconic."

"I don't know what that means."

He chuckled. "I'm not sure I do either." He took another swig of the wine and passed her the bottle. She took it without protest.

"How's your ass?"

"Sore." She smiled, but still looked like she was ready to cry.

"You look like you've been crying."

She looked out toward the fog gathered on the lake. "Why do they call this place Furnace Lake?"

"Obsession and insanity."

"What does that even mean?"

"Well, this is Ohio's idea of a resort town. Resort towns don't happen unless there are people to visit them and spend money there. As it happens, there's a town about twenty miles to the south called Milltown. Its main industry, at one point, was steel. So one of them came to this lake while the sun was setting and glowing orange like a blast furnace and they decided to name it Furnace Lake. It's a totally horrible, unromantic, disgusting name."

"I agree. It does sound warm though."

"But most people are only here in the summer. It seems like a furnace is the last thing you'd want to think about on a sweltering summer day."

"You might be right. Do you stay here in the summer?"

"Usually. Unless I'm teaching summer classes."

"Do you plan on doing that this year?"

"Probably not. I don't really need the money like I used to. That's really the only reason any professor gives up his or her summer."

"Doesn't sound fun."

"So, yeah, I'll probably head up here the week after finals. Would you be interested in joining me?" He didn't even know why he asked that.

She rolled her eyes. "That's a little too far in the future."

"I know. I don't even know why I asked. I've had a lot of fun today. I guess that's why. You've been very... kind to me."

"You act like that doesn't happen much."

"Well, not in that way. It's been over twenty years since I've had sex."

She reached out and patted his knee. "No it hasn't. It's only been like two hours."

"True. I guess I can't argue with that. Now the clock starts all over again."

"You did good after that long of a layoff."

"Thanks."

"Actually you did good period."

"Thanks more."

"Do you want to talk about it?"

"About what?"

"You fuck the same way you seem to live."

"What does that mean?"

"Like somebody who has something really wrong with them."

"Hm... what about you?"

"This isn't about me. Besides, I'm just a nineteen-year-old girl with a healthy sexual appetite. I could have landed some boy from the school and convinced him to come back to my parents' empty house for the weekend and fuck my brains out like a nineteen-year-old boy and it would have been like getting fucked by a nineteen-year-old boy. I like someone who's seen a little more. Thought about it a little more. *Planned* for it a little more. See, I didn't really have to tell you anything I wanted and you gave me a pretty nice day. So... wanna talk about it or not?"

He took another drink from the bottle. Followed by another. And suddenly he was almost blubbering. It seemed difficult to draw his next breath. He'd spent so much time just trying not to think about it that it never really occurred to him that he might actually talk to someone else about it. There was a period of time when he felt like he should probably go see a psychiatrist but he thought he was coping with it well enough on his own.

"Maybe."

"It'll make you feel better."

"I doubt that."

"Then it'll make you feel something."

"Where do I start?"

"Start with where things started to go bad."

That Was the Beginning of Bad

The miscarriage or the accident. Where to begin?

Start with the miscarriage. That was the beginning of bad. The accident was more of a worsening.

Heidi was pregnant and they weren't ready for it but they were still happy. The doctor told them she was pregnant with twins — one girl and one boy — and they knew they definitely weren't ready for *that* but, in a way, they were even happier. They had talked about having children, although they thought it would be something that would happen around the time they turned thirty. When Heidi got pregnant, she was twenty-four and Steve was twenty-six. They'd only planned on having two children and, ideally, they would be a girl and a boy. This would, in a way, be like getting it over with in one fell swoop. Then they could focus on their academic careers and child raising. *Focus.* It was something they'd both been lacking. If they had kids, they could stop trying to figure out who it was they wanted to be. They would have it handed to them. They would be parents and everything else would be secondary.

She was seven months along when Steve took her to the emergency room with swollen feet and bleeding. She'd had a couple of scares earlier on and had always been told everything was just fine. They were just overreacting. Their doctor had assured him that was perfectly normal for first time parents. Steve wasn't very worried.

From the moment the doctor inspected Heidi's stomach for the heartbeats there was nothing but worry. The next several hours were a steady ratcheting of that worry until it escalated to panic and then soul crushing grief.

He supposed the acceptance never came for either of them.

Heidi was in the hospital for a couple more days to let her recover and make sure everything was physically okay with her. From the day they returned home, to the tiny apartment Steve still lived in, he felt like he was in the unique and terrible position of trying to make Heidi feel better while dealing with his own grief. Meaning he tried not to be very open with his grief. Maybe it would have been better if he had but there was part of trying to feign normalcy that he liked. If he hadn't been the one to do it, life would have become unbearable. To Heidi, this was seen as something cold and callous. He didn't care about her. He didn't care about anything.

They argued a lot. He tried not to. He did a lot of tongue biting.

But there were only so many attacks he could take before breaking down and fighting back. And maybe, sometimes, his return attacks were overly vicious. He was doing everything he could.

Heidi dropped out of the master's program.

Not to worry. She needed a little more time before dealing with that kind of mental strain.

She stopped going to her job at the library.

Not to worry. He was an assistant professor so they had a steady income. It wasn't much but their living expenses were almost non-existent and their parents helped out, probably because they felt sorry for them.

She stopped getting out of bed. Stopped cleaning the house or herself. Steve suggested she see someone. She accused him of calling her crazy. Asked why he'd married her if he thought she was a psycho. Arguing was pointless. He would just leave. Go to a bar for a couple of hours while she cooled off or drive the half hour to his parents and sleep in his childhood bedroom. Few things were more humiliating than that.

The next spring he returned home from his last class of the semester and it was like Heidi had become someone else. They had a good summer. She smiled more. Was completely manic, in a good way, on some days, and they had lots and lots of sex. There was an almost frenzied quality to it. Toward the end of the summer, he realized she wasn't her old self at all. She had merely filled herself with some kind of obsessive optimism. Many times she mentioned "trying again." Steve told her there wasn't anything wrong with him and she wasn't using any birth control so, as far he was concerned, every time he came they were "trying again."

But nothing happened.

He was secretly relieved by this. He felt like, if there was anything good that came from the miscarriage, it was that they weren't ready for one kid, let alone two. It was a reprieve. He wasn't really one to believe in signs. He knew it was just biology and rotten luck but if either of them was the type to believe in signs, that would have been their mantra: "It was probably for the best. Maybe we weren't ready anyway." And while that kind of belief was something Steve had always seen as a sign of mental weakness, he was starting to realize that was exactly *why* people believed in those sorts of things. To keep themselves sane. Shouldering all the knowledge, all the *burden* of something like that was maddening.

Once he realized she didn't see it as sex, just babymaking, he started to lose interest.

They started arguing again.

She started going out with friends, girls she'd gone to high school and college with.

Steve felt like things were falling apart all over again. He was going to work to fix the relationship but the miscarriage was a trauma he didn't want to have to go through ever again. He made an appointment with a urologist, lied and said he was ten years older, told him he already had three kids, and got a vasectomy. He wasn't going to tell Heidi about it. If he could get her through this "trying again" phase then maybe they'd go to a fertility doctor and, if she were able to have children, he would be sterile. Therefore he could be the one to feel guilty about it. Maybe talk her into adopting a child.

Who was he kidding? She had been staying out all night and he was pretty sure she was fucking at least one other person, possibly more. He wanted to either start over with the old Heidi or someone else completely. Or not at all.

Less than a week after getting the vasectomy she changed again. Less frenzied. Less manic. More like her old self. And affectionate. She stopped mentioning anything about trying again. Maybe Steve's plaintive attempts to wait had finally taken hold. He thought she had even started taking her birth control pills again.

That winter – Friday, December 7, specifically – they went to dinner in Cincinnati. On the way home they hit a patch of black ice and crashed into a tree. Steve remembered sliding off the road clearly, but everything that came after that was a combination of hazy memory, his police report, and the newspaper articles he'd read against his better judgment.

The car slid off the road and into a tree. The car was totaled. He and Heidi were nearly totaled. But conscious. The car's engine was completely silent, the interior awash with beeping sounds and flashing lights. He looked over at Heidi. Her head was covered in blood. Her breath was shallow. He kept asking if she was okay. And she kept looking in the back seat and saying they had to take care of the kids. Telling her she was delusional or crazy was the furthest thing from Steve's mind. Yes, yes, he said, we'll take care of the kids but we need to find someone. We need to get help. And she said that wasn't what they needed. They didn't need help. The children needed to be buried. They were beyond help. There was a brief moment where he wondered if she was talking about the miscarriage. Maybe she was confused. He told her that they had already buried the children, didn't she remember? She told him that wasn't right. They never saw what happened to them. Anything could have happened to them. And besides they weren't buried they were cremated. That's right, Steve remembered. They were cremated. We have the urn in a kitchen cabinet. Yes, she said and wiped blood out of her eyes. And we need to make sure these get taken care of by us. She told him to get the boy and she would get the girl. He was amazed they were able to get out of the car. Amazed they were able to move at all. Heidi opened the back door and feigned taking a child out of a car seat. Steve did the same. She took off walking through the woods, through the slushy mud that was winter in Ohio, and it occurred to Steve that they were much closer to the cabin than they were the apartment and that was quite likely where they were going. The coroner would later say he thought it was nearly impossible for them, especially her, to do what it was they had done. Even the police report was free of any description of them wandering through the woods, as though he had completely blacked out during that period. They arrived at the lake and continued to walk to their cabin. Once at the cabin Heidi demanded he go retrieve a shovel, two if they had them. He went to the small utility shed, unlocked it, and removed a shovel. There was another one in there, but the thought of Heidi digging anything made him nauseous. He returned with the shovel and she said they didn't need to dig two holes, they could just bury them together. He began digging. Told her she should go up to the porch and sit down. She said she was okay, she wanted to hold their babies. While he dug, she stood in the moonlight of the crystal clear night and stared out at the lake. What was she thinking? He knew she wasn't in her right mind, but what was going through her head at that moment? He dug quickly. The ground wasn't frozen and it was still damp which made it that much easier. He dug down maybe a little more than a foot. His head was swimming and spinning and he felt like he could collapse at any moment. He told her he thought it was ready. She bent down on her knees and placed the imaginary children in the hole and said something that sounded like a prayer. Then she collapsed face first in the hole. He pulled her out, lay down beside the hole, and cradled her in his arm, her head resting on his shoulder. The way they used to sleep when they had first gotten married.

Just Gone

"Can I have one of those?" Steve pointed at Ashley's pack of cigarettes. She handed them to him. He lit one, fought back a cough, and said, "The next thing I remember was sitting in the back of an ambulance. I kept asking them what happened to Heidi and they wouldn't tell me. That's when I knew she was dead. By the time we got to the hospital, she wasn't even hooked up to anything. Just gone. She was probably gone before they even got there."

Steve thought he would cry if he ever told that story but he wasn't.

"Was that the first time you've ever told that to anyone... besides the police?"

He nodded slowly. "I think it felt good. I never realized how crazy it sounded."

She kind of laughed. "It did sound pretty crazy. And sad."

"Definitely sad."

"And your life just stopped then, huh?"

"Well, I didn't think it had at the time but now... I guess looking at all the wasted years, you could probably say that."

Then he did cry. She took the cigarette out of his hand and crushed it out on the arm of the chair. She placed a hand on the back of his head, pulled him up out of the chair, and walked him to bed.

When he woke up the next morning she was gone.

He Found Himself Completely Enervated

He went back home as soon as he looked around and waited long enough to know she wasn't there and wasn't coming back.

For the next four months, he divided his time between his apartment and the college, just like always. He pulled her file at school and noticed she hadn't enrolled for the second semester at all. He emailed her. He didn't feel comfortable calling the number he had for her and didn't know if she would really want him to call her anyway. The cynical thought would have been that she got what she wanted and then decided to disappear but what could she have possibly gained from their encounter? He had certainly had a good time but their last bout had nearly left her in tears. He hadn't given her any money or promises or anything. Maybe he'd just freaked her out. Or maybe she had realized she'd made a big mistake and decided to take off. She could have had someone come and pick her up or maybe she took a bus or something. He couldn't exactly ask around about her at school without looking like a creep. Maybe he would have approached one of her friends but he hadn't really paid attention to who she hung around with, if anyone. He was usually focused on her.

For the first month, the elation of their meeting and the hope she would contact *him* sustained him. In February and March – the last couple months of guaranteed cold weather – he found himself completely enervated. This was usually a bad time of year for him anyway. One can only take so many months of gray, miserable weather. He used to come home from class, make a small but tasty meal from scratch, and spend the evening reading and listening to music. If these things didn't make him authentically happy, they at least got him very close to the real thing. Representations of happiness. Then he would usually find some pornography on the Internet or jerk off to the thought of one of his students before falling asleep. But now he didn't even feel like doing that.

He told himself he had had something and let it get away but he knew he was kidding himself. What did he have? Ashley was just a girl who wanted to sleep with one of her professors. They did that for a few hours, she probably realized it wasn't what she thought it would be, and decided to bolt. Probably even had her boyfriend from back home pick her up. In a way, it was hard not to be mad at her, but he knew if she called or contacted him, he wouldn't show her any trace of anger.

By the middle of April, a gorgeous spring had finally arrived. When classes ended at the end of May, Steve was looking forward to packing up and heading to the cabin for the summer. The week before he left, he had the dream every night. There were minor variations. In a couple of them, Heidi was Ashley. In one of them, Steve dug the grave and the grave became a bed and he fucked Ashley in it but halfway through she became Heidi and Heidi was rotting and wearing her bridal veil and ejaculating sperm from her nipples. Steve decided when he came back, if the dreams hadn't gotten any better, he would finally see a psychiatrist, to see if he could prescribe something to help him sleep more than anything else.

Most of the essentials were already at the cabin so all Steve had to pack were some clothes and groceries.

The Twin Dimples Just Above Her Waist

Steve opened the cabin door and stood there with a grocery bag in one hand and his keys in the other, thinking he hadn't had to unlock the door but also thinking maybe it was something he'd done so many times in the past he just didn't remember doing it. He pocketed the keys. The cabin didn't seem as stale as it usually did. Maybe that was because of his winter tryst. That was how he had decided to think of it. A "tryst." It made it sound more festive, which he guessed it was. It was the fallout that was depressing. Of course even that was relatively small compared to the fallout that had been the last twenty plus years of his life. He'd decided to let the lease on his apartment go when it ran out this October. He had plenty of money to buy a house. Maybe he'd even join a dating site or go out to bars or something. Hell, maybe he'd even grow the balls to ask one of the several single female professors he knew out. Opportunities like Ashley were not going to come around every year. So far the odds, apparently, were more like once every twenty years. He didn't know if he'd be around when another presented itself.

He sat the bag of groceries on the kitchen table and felt bad about having relegated Ashley to an "opportunity."

He heard footsteps and turned around quickly.

Ashley stood in the door of the bedroom.

"Don't be mad," she said.

Steve didn't know *what* to say. He felt like he was blushing, trying to find the right words before opening his mouth. He'd thought about Ashley so much over the past few months, that his emotions had spanned the entire spectrum more than once.

He gripped the counter and looked away from her. "I'm not sure what to say. Why...?"

"Why am I here?"

"Um... yeah, I guess. And how?"

"I thought I would surprise you."

"I'm... definitely surprised."

"And happy?" She smiled and approached him.

Fuck it, he thought. He opened his arms and accepted her, pulled her into him and wrapped her tightly. "Very happy."

"We can pick up right where we left off."

He didn't waste any time. He walked her over to the couch, bent her over the arm, peeled down her jeans and underwear, and pushed himself in. It didn't last long. He tried to force all the questions out of his head. Looking down at her back muscles writhing under her skin tight t-shirt and the twin dimples just above her waist made it not that hard at all.

They Already Acted Married

When they finished, she stood up, pulled up her pants, and adjusted her bra. Steve went to the car to grab the rest of the stuff. Out by the car, he took a second to stop and look around. Summer was finally here. The woody smells and sounds immediately made him feel more restful. He saw other families in the distance, in the yards of their cabins, some of them barbecuing. There were even a couple of boats out on the lake. Steve liked it here. If he didn't he would have probably sold the place immediately after Heidi died.

He went back into the cabin and found that Ashley had already put the groceries in the refrigerator.

"Very domestic," he said.

She shrugged. "Well, you know..."

He looked at her for a second. "No. I really don't. I have a lot of questions for you."

"But you *are* glad I'm here, right? Even after shooting your wad in me? Which is running out even as we speak."

"Lovely."

"It's mostly your fault."

"Agreed. Hungry?"

"Starved."

Steve decided to save the questions for dinner. He didn't feel like dragging the grill out so he just decided to make something in the kitchen. Maybe some kind of chicken stir fry. He reached into the pantry and grabbed the bag of rice.

"What do you need from the fridge?"

"Maybe just the chicken. Unless you put the teriyaki sauce in there too."

She handed him the chicken. "The sauce should be in the cabinet."

Steve turned back to the cabinet and was overcome with a case of the shakes. It was eerie. They'd spent one day fucking and had now been together only a few minutes and they already acted married. He liked that feeling. It surprised him.

He poured some water in a pan, dumped in a couple handfuls of rice and a bit of olive oil, and set it on the stove. She put a bottle of beer in front of him.

He chopped the onions and the peppers and then didn't really have anything to do until the rice started boiling. He couldn't wait until they were sitting down. If he did, he wouldn't ask her at all. He'd just fall into whatever groove she wanted him to fall into.

"So how long have you been here?"

She was cutting the chicken and looked up. "Huh?"

He nodded at the bottle of beer. "That's a Budweiser. I brought Heineken. Also, the stuff I brought wouldn't have been this cold."

"Just since last night. I promise."

"What made you want to come back? I notice you dropped out of school."

"Yeah. I guess I was just thinking about you. Can we talk about it later, maybe?"

"Sure. I hope it's nothing too serious."

"Just family stuff."

"I might not be able to empathize."

She smiled and took a sip of his beer.

"How did you get in, anyway?"

"The window in the bathroom. I popped the screen out and the window was unlatched."

"That window's tiny."

"I'm not very big myself."

He still didn't see how it was possible. But maybe the window had become smaller in his mind. He told her he had to pee and she asked if he didn't believe her. He laughed and said of course he did but, once in the bathroom, he did find himself studying the tiny window. He still didn't see how it was possible but it would probably be rude to measure her.

Everything Was Made of Lead

A half hour later they sat at the small table in the kitchen, their dinners half eaten. They had made casual conversation. He'd asked her why she had dropped out of school and what she'd been up to and she gave him back a steady stream of what were probably lies. Then he asked her how long she'd really been staying here and she stammered and her eyes hardened somewhat. While he was in the bathroom, he'd noticed most of his supply of toilet paper was gone. So she'd either cleaned up well or not made much of a mess in the first place, but she'd definitely been here for more than a night.

"I never left."

"What?" As happy as he was to have her in front of him, he

couldn't help but be a little angry with her.

"Yeah. That time this winter. I never left. I went for a walk and just kind of hid until I saw you leave."

"But why?"

"I told you. Family stuff."

"Fighting with your parents?"

"Something like that."

"You're going to have to stop being so cryptic."

"I don't know what that means."

"Maybe I should punish you."

"Oh. Are we still playing that game? I was going to humor you and let you play the husband and wife game but, to be honest, that was already getting a little boring."

"Get into the bedroom."

"But I'm not even finished eating."

"Now."

She stood up and made a mock pouting face.

"I really am mad at you, Ashley."

She stomped off into the bedroom. He tried to stand up to follow her but it felt like everything was made of lead. He forced himself to stand and was distantly aware of his body hitting the floor and then he wasn't aware of anything.

We Live Down Here Now

He dug the grave until it felt like every muscle had given out and he might fall down. He looked down at the grave and was pleased to see that it was as deep of one as any he'd remembered digging. The palms of his hands stung. He looked over his shoulder at the cabin. Expecting to see it darkened. But the lights were on and there were people inside. It was good that somebody still wanted it. He could hear distant laughter and music. See the silhouettes of people in the window.

He looked back at the grave. He couldn't see the bottom of it. A voice called from the grave but he couldn't see who it was coming from.

He got down on his hands and knees and then his stomach and

96

leaned his head into the grave. It was Heidi, calling to him.

"What are you doing up there?"

"I had to dig the grave. We have to bury the children. What are you doing down there? How did you get down there?"

She laughed. "We live down here now. The kids are already down here. You should join us."

He pulled himself with his arms, feeling the moist grass on his stomach, before sliding down the side of the grave. He was afraid he'd just fall in head first but it was angled more than he thought it was. Like a slide. He slid to the bottom. The grave was quite roomy. He looked around but didn't see any sign of Heidi and the children. He stood up. The grave leveled off but continued into the distance. The narrow earthen corridor surrounded him as he walked deeper into it.

It curved to the right and when he made the turn he had to shield his eyes against the glow that met him. It was like a giant fire. He thought he could make out Heidi in the middle of the fire, a waist-high child to either side of her.

"I don't want to go any farther," he said.

"You have to. Your family's here."

He cautiously stepped toward them. Gradually his eyes adjusted to the light and he could begin to see the children as something other than black shapes. One was a girl and one was a boy. They looked happy and clear-eyed. Heidi wore her wedding veil. As he drew closer, he noticed her nipples had elongated and reached the mouth of each child.

Steve stopped.

"Come on," Heidi said.

"No. I can't."

Steve took off running in the opposite direction but the corridor was gone and he found himself running into loose dirt, trying to move his arms and legs to kick out of it, but nothing was moving and he was suffocating.

Slit Rider

"Finally," a male voice said.

Steve opened his eyes to see a hideously ugly guy taking his hand away from Steve's mouth. The first thing Steve thought was that he'd been holding his nose closed to try and get him to wake up. The guy might have been a teenager, or recently a teenager, but there was something a lot older looking about him. He had a tattoo on the front of his neck that said SLIT RIDER in vaguely gothic lettering.

"Who the fuck are you?" Steve asked.

The man stood up and said, "I'm Slit Rider, fucker."

Steve's heart raced. He looked down at himself. He was tied to a chair. He wasn't wearing any clothes.

"What the fuck is going on?" he asked. "Why are you in my house? Where's Ashley?"

The man laughed. "Ashley's dead, stooge. Ashley's been dead a long time and something. Reborn as Sharon X. Now she's here. Now she's mine. Two hands. Two feet. Electric brain."

Steve took a deep breath and closed his eyes. He didn't know what was going on. The only thing he could think was that this was maybe Ashley's boyfriend or something and he had apparently found out what he and Ashley had been doing and was upset. But Steve didn't know how to defend himself against that. He wasn't going to tell this jackass everything was Ashley's doing.

"Look," Steve said. "I don't know who you are or what you want but if you untie me now and just leave, I won't press any charges."

The man (Steve had a hard time thinking of him as Slit Rider) leaned into Steve. He reeked of whiskey, smoke, and maybe something else. Some foul underlying odor. "That's a good thought box, Steves. I don't know why I didn't think of that and everything else with the laughing. Horseplay." Now behind Steve, the man tugged on a couple of the ropes. Then Steve felt his hands around his neck. The man squeezed until Steve blacked out.

Almost Everything in the Cabin Was on the Verge of Falling Apart

This time when he came to there wasn't anyone in front of him. The room was dark. He heard loud music that sounded like clanging metal and a drum machine coming from the next room. It sounded like there were also a lot of people in there. Raucous shouts and laughter. Steve tried to rock the chair back and forth until he realized if he actually managed to tip it over he would probably still be tied to the chair, only on the floor and with the ropes quite possibly binding him in an even more uncomfortable position.

Unless he could get the chair to break. Almost everything in the cabin was on the verge of falling apart. If he could get the chair to break, it might create some slack in the rope and then he could get out through a window and go to one of the neighbor's houses. He needed to call the police. The people in the other room were making so much noise he was kind of surprised one of the neighbors hadn't called the police already.

He made a motion like standing up straight to see if he could weaken the chair at all. He heard it creak but it gave only fractionally. He might have been able to inflict more damage if he didn't feel so weak. He assumed Ashley or Sharon X or whoever had slipped something into his beer. Maybe even the food. But probably the beer. It was Bud so it pretty much tasted like shit anyway. He wouldn't have been able to tell.

He continued to slowly grind against the chair. Hoping it would give a little more before trying to drive himself into the ground with it. If he was going to do that, he wanted to be pretty sure it was going to break. He listened to the sounds coming from the other room. He was still trying to figure out why this was happening and was hoping they would be talking about it. Maybe give him some kind of clue that could become a psychological advantage.

The music *was* really loud and sounded intolerable. If they *were* having a party, he didn't know who partied to this kind of music. The only words he could make out were what sounded like a woman talking about "shoulder pads" and "conquering the moon." Not a lot of help. Those phrases were repeated over and over. There weren't any other discernible words. Someone else just shouted "Wheee!" continuously like they were on the world's longest slide or roller coaster or something. He guessed there were at least five or six people in the room. It was possible that Slit

Rider and Ashley were the only people who knew he was in here. So he decided to see if he could go ahead and rock the chair onto the floor. If it broke then he'd be able to get out through the window. If it didn't then he would shout for help. He highly doubted it but supposed it was possible someone in the other room would help him. He thought about the gun he had hidden away in one of the kitchen cupboards. Wondered if they'd found it yet.

He didn't know how much real danger he was in anyway. So far, other than drugging him and choking him to the point of unconsciousness, nobody had done anything to seriously hurt him. Maybe they didn't *want* to hurt him. What kind of motive was there anyway? If Slit Rider really was Ashley's jealous boyfriend or ex-boyfriend or whatever, he would have probably just beaten the hell out of Steve and called it a day. Maybe taken Ashley with him. Ashley had been using Steve for a place to stay and, he supposed, it was entirely possible Slit Rider had been staying here with her. So maybe they wanted money. Steve had plenty of money. He had no problems with giving them whatever they asked for. Of course he would go immediately to the police once he was able.

He heard something that sounded like a window breaking and wondered, once again, what the fuck they were doing in there.

He gritted his teeth and began rocking the chair back and forth, more and more violently, until he hit the ground and was... lying on his side on the ground and tied to a chair.

Fuck.

It Seemed No One Heard Him Collapse

With all the commotion going on in the other room, it seemed no one heard him collapse. He thought once again about crying out but didn't see how that would help anything. It would probably just serve to infuriate Slit Rider even further. If he had been furious before. Steve wasn't really sure. It was kind of hard to gauge any type of feeling from the man. There was something off about him but Steve couldn't figure out what it was. It looked like he was missing something.

He continued to struggle against the chair and the rope.

At least an hour passed before anyone entered the room. Slit Rider was the first one in. He turned the lights on in the room.

"What the fucks!?" he shouted. He walked over to Steve and uprighted the chair. "You're going to want to sees this. Take a magic looks, astronaut."

Ashley was the next to enter the room, followed by two more men. One of them was missing an arm. The other one had an eyepatch. The one with the eyepatch said, "I am not ready yet." Then he vomited on the floor and said, "Now I am ready."

Ashley walked slowly toward Steve and sat on his lap. The three men stood in front of the bed, about a foot in front of Ashley, and began removing their clothes. Ashley was doing the same although in a much slower, more seductive manner.

"Ashley," Steve tried to whisper in her ear. At that point, the room was so quiet while the men waited for her to take her clothes off that they probably heard him. Maybe there was a lot of blood pounding in their ears or something.

Halfway through unbuttoning her shirt, Ashley turned so that her face was barely an inch from Steve's. "I am *not* Ashley. Not anymore. Ashley is dead. Now I am Sharon X. Slit Rider has baptized me and I was born again. Born from space, not a mother. Mothers are gross."

Steve tried to find whatever it was he'd seen in Ashley's eyes before. Maybe he hadn't seen anything. Maybe he'd been so blinded by the prospect and the actual act of sex that it didn't really matter what he'd seen in those eyes. Maybe she was really high on something.

"Come on," he said. "You're throwing your life away with these people."

"At least I had one to throw away."

That remark cut deeply. He felt like she'd listened to his story without any sympathy whatsoever. Listened to it for ammunition more than anything, possibly.

She stood up and turned fully in front of him. She finished unbuttoning her shirt and let it drop to the floor. She unbuttoned her jeans and peeled those down. She had an "X" tattooed on her bare pubis.

"Watch this if you doubt Slit Rider's space magic."

Steve had the feeling he was about ready to watch a whole lot of things he didn't really want to see so wasn't sure what Ashley was specifically talking about.

She lay on her back on the bed. Eyepatch and One Arm went to either side of the bed. Their cocks were large and erect. She took one in each hand. She spread her legs and Slit Rider lowered his head between them. He dived in like an animal, licking and slurping. Steve thought about the deposit he'd made there only a few hours ago and wasn't sure if he was satisfied or nauseous. One Arm leaned into Ashley and she took his penis into her mouth.

"Ashley. Sharon X. Whatever. Why are you doing this?"

She took her mouth away. "Why shouldn't I be? I've known these guys longer than I knew you when you did this to me."

Slit Rider hopped off the bed and pounced in front of Steve. He belched in his face and threw his arms up in the air like he'd achieved some victory.

"Now I've got your sperms in my belly! Dead sperms with nothing ever in them! Dead sperms! Dead sperms! Dead sperms!"

He was leaping up and down. Steve couldn't help but notice Slit Rider was erect also. And that his penis was huge. Slit Rider grabbed his penis and began slapping Steve's cheeks with it. Then he turned and leaped between Ashley's legs, thrusting quickly. She was now taking turns sucking Eyepatch and One Arm and, when she didn't have a penis in her mouth, grinning at Steve. A few seconds later, Slit Rider thrust harder and cried out. Steve thought he shouted "Rocket" but he might have misheard him. Everything the guy said seemed to be something like gibberish so he figured it probably didn't really matter anyway.

One Arm took his turn next.

Slit Rider left the bed to stand next to Steve and poke him in the face with his index finger, as though testing his reality. Steve fantasized about biting it off.

One Arm was finished even faster than Slit Rider and Eyepatch took his turn.

When he finished, Ashley pulled her knees up to her chest and rocked back slightly. That was the first indication Steve had of what he might be in for. Slit Rider was giggling. He searched around the clothes on the floor until he came up with a belt. He forced Steve's mouth open by poking him in the eye. Then he wrapped the belt around Steve's head. Steve closed his mouth as far as he could, teeth pressing into the leather, but he didn't get it closed all the way. Slit Rider and Eyepatch lowered the chair until Steve's back was on the ground. Ashley was suddenly above his head, lowering her glistening vagina to his mouth.

The semen came out in clumpy, warm drops. Steve closed his eyes, thinking that might help him to avoid throwing up. Not that throwing up the sperm of three men was unappealing, he just thought that, with the belt in his mouth, it might make things even worse.

"You like that?" Slit Rider was whispering into his ear. "All that sperm's filled with little space babies. You're going to be just like the Virgins Mary. Shooting out babies without us having to fuck you in the mouth hole."

They left him on his back and went back to their partying, music turned up, the smell of smoke wafting from the main room. Steve thought he was so tired and had released so much adrenaline that he might actually be able to go to sleep but they'd left the light on and it was shining right into his eyes. Maybe two hours later Ashley came back into the room and lay next to him on the floor. Her hand went to his penis and he told himself he wasn't going to get hard, that she repulsed him, but he got hard anyway.

"The problem with you is that you don't see anything."

"I don't see how you're in any condition to diagnose my problems. You're less than half my age and you might be insane."

"That's very hurtful. I indulged you, didn't I?"

He didn't say anything.

"That one night. I told you you could do anything you wanted to with me and I thought you did. I thought I let you. I thought I let you indulge. Maybe you should have killed me. Maybe that was really what I wanted. What would you have done if I'd told you that was what I wanted? That I had always felt dead inside and that I wanted you to kill me and fuck my corpse. That I didn't really have a family, no one to go back to, no one to miss me. That I'd already withdrawn from college. Would you have done it?"

He didn't answer. How could he? Of course he wouldn't have done it. But was that what she wanted to hear?

"You don't see anything that matters. You think women have to be brides or whores. You saw me as something innocent, didn't you? And then you saw me as a whore. But I bet you started thinking about something more than just fucking me that first time I gave you head in the car. Probably because you felt guilty. That's probably why you told me that story about your family."

"Not family. Wife."

"Oh, right, because the children didn't exist. They were imaginary. And you're wife was crazy. Did you know she *was* actually pregnant with twins?"

"Not mine. And good job. You looked it up. Thanks for believing me."

"Of course not. They couldn't have been, could they? Jesus, you're rock hard."

He didn't say anything.

"I met Slit Rider right before I came out here with you. That was one of the reasons I came with you. You were normalcy. I thought you were the most normal person I'd ever met. And I wanted to taste it. I wanted to see if that was something I could be."

"I'm not that normal."

"But you are. Don't you see that? Don't you realize that's what normal is? Everyone has problems. Everyone has a shitty life. But people who embrace that and do something with the misery are seen as the abnormal ones. And the people who apply normalcy like a camouflage suit are seen as the normal ones. And I figured out why this is. Because we're a democratic society, Steve. And when there are more fucked up people than not fucked up people, that becomes the status quo. The mentally healthy – people like Slit Rider – are outcast. That's why we have to make our own society."

She jerked him vigorously and he couldn't help coming. He didn't say anything else. He just closed his eyes and nearly wept. He was hoping they were just thieves but now he was starting to think they were some kind of death cult or just psychopathic or out of their heads on something and that scared him a lot more.

"Listen to Slit Rider. He'll teach you that everyone is a beautiful creature from space. There is no normal. There are no mothers, no whores, no men, no women. Wielders of cock and pussy. That's all we are."

She dipped her fingers in his semen and spent several minutes sliding them in and out of his nostrils.

Slayer

He must have fallen asleep or passed out eventually. He didn't remember her leaving the room. He didn't remember much of anything. There were the party sounds in the other room and he just tried to find a comfortable bass line and focus his attention on that and the next thing he knew the room was filled with morning sunlight and Slit Rider was jerking his chair up and throwing Steve's wallet at him and shouting "No pins. No pins. No pins."

Luckily, Ashley came in after him to translate.

"We need your PIN number, Steve."

He laughed.

Yesterday, before being forced to drink the semen of three men after watching them fuck a girl he'd become fond of, he would have given them the number easily. Hell, he probably would have driven them to the ATM just to avoid further trouble. Now they had put certain things into perspective. He'd been humiliated and terrified. But that wasn't it. He'd also had it made painfully clear to him that he had basically died a long time ago. If he got out of this, he would make some changes, sure, but he was finished emasculating himself. And he still wasn't sure if they were actually homicidal or just goofballs.

Steve laughed, he couldn't help it, and said, "I'm not giving you the number. It's private. It's personal. Feel free to steal anything that isn't nailed down. But I'm finished volunteering information." He looked at Ashley. "You've been irresponsible with it so far."

Something like wild rage shot through Slit Rider's eyes – shot through his whole face – before it returned to that creepy blank potato and he stood up straight.

"Bring in Slayer!" he shouted.

Steve didn't know what to expect. He thought maybe Slit Rider was talking about One Arm or Eyepatch, since Steve hadn't caught their names previously. Or maybe another man, large and brutish, someone fitting of the name Slayer.

In walked a very young girl. She couldn't have been more than twelve or thirteen.

"You know what to do, Slayer."

The girl walked in front of Steve and got down on her knees. He tried to cross his legs but he couldn't. At least he figured he wasn't going to get an erection. There was nothing about that particular age bracket that turned him on. But then the thought that he *shouldn't* be aroused was slightly arousing him so he had to focus on the other people in the room. How much he hated them. How awkward this whole situation was.

Slit Rider had some kind of smartphone in his hand, aiming it at Steve and the girl.

"We'll gets it all on camera. Big crime. This."

Steve looked at the girl and said, "Don't."

Her head paused in its descent to his crotch. At this point, he was just happy she understood a word he said.

"Is that all you want? The pin number to my debit card? I don't really have much in there."

"It's tip of the iceberg of dicks."

"Also, this would probably be more of a crime if I wasn't in restraints. I mean, what? She's going to give me head and I'm not going to be aroused and I'm not going to come and then you're going to show this video to somebody and prove to them that I was held against my will while somebody else forced this underage girl to perform oral sex on me. How is that a good idea?"

"He's got smart brains. Hold ons, Slayer. Don't move around on its."

Slit Rider left the room and came back with Steve's gun. He was hoping they hadn't found it. It was a fully loaded Glock. Steve kept it around the cabin only as a last ditch thing. Maybe at one point he'd bought it to convince himself he wasn't suicidal like some people keep a bottle of booze or a pack of cigarettes in their homes to prove to themselves they're no longer addicted. Slit Rider handed the gun to Ashley and started untying Steve.

"Now you will be criminal," Slit Rider said.

The ropes dropped and Steve immediately felt tingling in his arms and legs. He'd had a grand vision of the ropes dropping away and him springing into action but, if he tried to move now, he would just fall on his face.

At least he was able to twist his legs and penis away when the girl bent for it.

Ashley, possibly mistaking this for an escape attempt, pulled the trigger.

Part of the girl's face exploded outward and blood sprayed Steve's chest. If the bullet hit him, he was unaware. Now he had to move. He lunged for the door of the room and, as he feared, went sprawling face first. He was also aware that he was screaming. And maybe pissing.

"What do you want?! What do you want?!" He thought he said this a hundred more times.

"Shit," Ashley said.

"No bigs," Slit Rider said.

Steve hoped maybe a neighbor had heard the gunshot. Maybe they thought he'd finally decided to off himself.

"We need to get out of here," Ashley said.

"Calm calm."

"Grab Parachute and Tram and let's get the *fuck* out of here."

Slit Rider slapped Ashley and she shot Steve in the back of his right leg. It felt like a lead weight and then nothing. Maybe that was the beauty of shock.

Slit Rider grabbed Steve around the wrist and dragged him into the main room. Ashley ran to the door and said, "Jesus, Slitty, they already took off. Fuckers probably left with the first shot."

The only thing Steve had the capacity to do in the way of self-defense was roll. He began rolling to his left, not really knowing where his ultimate goal was. His legs felt like sandbags attached to his body. Slit Rider leapt over him and placed a foot on his waist. Slit Rider threw his hands up in the air.

"Don't you sees, Sharon X? This is how it's meant. We are ready for space. Ready for space!"

"What the fuck are you talking about?"

"Shoot me in the face. Do it now!"

"I'm not going to shoot you in the face. We're not meant to die."

"Not die. Space!"

Slit Rider moved toward Ashley. With Slit Rider's foot gone, Steve began trying to army crawl. He thought he would try for the bathroom. See what happened then. At least there was a door with a lock on it. He didn't think he had any hope of making it out the window and knew there was no way he could make it past Slit Rider and Ashley to get to the front door. He stopped to look back at Slit Rider and Ashley. Slit Rider had his hands around Ashley's and the gun and then there was a loud crack and he hit the ground. Since Steve was the only person besides herself Ashley hadn't killed, he crawled for the bathroom even faster, almost expecting a bullet to find its way into his head. Before pulling himself into the bathroom, he looked back and saw Ashley standing over Slit Rider's body with something like reverence in her eyes. She wasn't crying anymore. She still held the gun in her hand.

Steve closed the door to the bathroom.

He heard another shot.

Bury the Children in the Yard

Steve didn't know how long he stayed in the bathroom. Didn't know what he was waiting for. Sirens maybe. He either dozed off or passed out from the pain. While he was out he had the dream. This time it was different only in that it didn't have any children in it. He and Heidi still wandered away from the car after the accident but when they got to the cabin she collapsed onto the ground and told him to bury her because she was killing him. She said she was already dead. Had been for a long time. He did what he was told and didn't wake up until he miscalculated with the shovel and brought it down on his foot. By the time he awoke, the pain had traveled all the way up his leg.

There still wasn't any sign of the police.

He tried to stand up and managed it with relative ease. He looked at his leg. The side of his leg had a line of flesh that had been torn away. The bullet must have only grazed him. He felt stupid and cowardly. Maybe his leg had still been asleep when Ashley shot at him. If so, that meant he might have been able to do something about the scene in the living room.

He walked out into the living room, the smell of blood and shit hitting his nostrils.

Slit Rider still lay on the floor. Ashley lay crosswise on top of him. The gun lay on the floor a few feet away.

He found one of Ashley's cigarettes, took it out to the front porch, and lit it.

The sun was just going down, the sky was clear, and the lake glowed a hellish orange.

He was surprisingly calm. This was the second most traumatic thing that had happened to him and, in a way, he didn't even feel a part of it. He owned the cabin where it took place. He'd had sex with Ashley but what did any of it have to do with him? What would happen if he *did* call the police? He would be questioned, for sure. But he was convinced he wouldn't be found guilty of anything. Which he wasn't. And then what? And then life would go on exactly as it had before.

He might as well be one of the corpses in the house.

He stayed on the porch until night bloomed, black and moonless.

He went into the house and cleaned his wound and bandaged his leg. He thought about burning down the cabin. But that didn't seem poetic enough. He went out to the tool shed and found his shovel, probably the same one he'd used to bury his imaginary children. He could now hear some of the families around the lake, kids shouting, adult conversations. Laughter. Full lives. Where were they earlier? Maybe they were so turned inward they didn't hear much of anything happening around them. And maybe that was only because they were on vacation. In Steve's experience it seemed like most people paid way too much attention to things that didn't really have anything to do with them. Maybe that was it. Maybe they turned away when it was anything that might demand some kind of involvement and chose only to focus on minutiae.

Who knew?

Who knew much of anything?

Steve was sure he didn't. He was going to dig a hole. The sun would be coming up in about seven hours so he thought he had some time. Then he would drag the corpses from the house and put them in the hole. Then he would fill the hole and go into the cabin and clean up as best he could, but not perfectly. He didn't think he wanted to remove all the evidence of what had happened. He would know *some*thing had happened. He wouldn't tell anyone about it no matter how much he might want to. It would be his.

He broke the ground with the shovel and some dark cloud broke within him, filling him with thunder and lightning and rain. He listened to the families around him play and continued to dig the hole.

Other Grindhouse Press Titles

#666 – *Satanic Summer*
by Andersen Prunty

#012 – *Return to Devil Town (Vampires in Devil Town Book Three)*
by Wayne Hixon

#011 – *Pray You Die Alone: Horror Stories*
by Andersen Prunty

#010 – *King of the Perverts*
by Steve Lowe

#009 – *Sunruined: Horror Stories*
by Andersen Prunty

#008 – *Bright Black Moon: Vampires in Devil Town Book Two*
by Wayne Hixon

#007 – *Hi I'm a Social Disease: Horror Stories*
by Andersen Prunty

#006 – *A Life On Fire*
by Chris Bowsman

www.ingramcontent.com/pod-product-compliance
Lightning Source LLC
Chambersburg PA
CBHW050420110726
47899CB00008B/2782